Better Off Dead

JA Wynters

Prologue

Before the end of my fucking world

6/5/2008
Ethan

I stare at the ceiling. When I became so lucky? No, it wasn't being born in a Vale or being in line to inherit a ridiculous fortune that I would not be able to spend in three lifetimes. It was the thought of what we just did, of what Hannah has gifted me. She squirms in my arms, and I turn to her.

I kiss her again. If I died right now, I'd die the happiest man in the world. Nothing tastes better than Hannah—nothing feels better than having her here in my arms, her sweaty naked body sticking to mine. The euphoria of savouring her. She belongs to me, but not in the way that everything else in the world has fallen into my lap. Hannah *wants* to be here with me. She's chosen it and that makes it so much sweeter, so much more satisfying.

Her lips brush mine again. Her head rests on my chest, and I know she feels the thrumming of my heart.

It beats for her alone.

As I wrap my hand around her shoulders and pull her closer to me, I think about the three years we've spent together. About how we both have our whole lives ahead of us, and that, with no uncertain clarity, there is no one in the world I'd rather spend it with.

But with that comes a slow, sinking dread that soon I'll have to leave, head to university, move on without her. Not if I can find a way to take her with me. Not if I can make her mine in the way that makes walking away feel like moving forward.

"You're suddenly very quiet."

"Just thinking."

"Don't hurt yourself." Her voice is teasing, and her lips curve into a smile against my chest.

"Can't make promises," I shoot back, grinning as she lightly punches my arm.

"What are you thinking about?"

"You, us."

"Us? Should I be worried?" She lifts herself, her beautiful eyes narrowing playfully. "You know too much."

"Just enough to go to the authorities if needed."

"We both know they won't believe you." She flutters her eyes innocently, and I crack a smile. She studies me for a second. "Seriously, what's going on?"

"Seriously? You've never been serious a day in your life."

She punches my side, and I chuckle. "Ethan."

I hesitate, sucking in a deep breath. How to phrase it without freaking her out. "Do you ever think about... the future?"

"The future? Like when the robots take over, or us?"

"You, me, robots. All of it."

"Ethan." She pokes my side, getting exasperated, and I catch her hand, holding it in mine.

"Fine. Us." I squeeze her hand gently. "Do you ever think about what it's going to be like after school? Where we'll be, what we'll do."

She tilts her head, considering. "I mean, yeah. We'll both go to uni, I'll become a teacher, you'll become... richer?"

"Not sure that's possible." I wiggle my eyebrows, and she huffs.

I turn my body to hers, feeling the heat. "It's just that the past three years... the way you make me feel. I don't want it to change."

She doesn't speak, instead tucks her head against my chest again, her body relaxing against me, the steady rhythm of her breathing matching mine.

I close my eyes, and memories flood my mind. The first time I decided to take a chance and cross the boundary from friends to more... I asked her out, fumbling over my words like a complete idiot, convinced she'd laugh in my face. Instead, she smiled—this shy, breathtaking smile—and said yes.

If I thought we were inseparable before we started dating, being her boyfriend gave me a whole new side of Hannah. Crossing that line, it changes everything, but also, somehow, nothing at all. Like, she's still the same person. Still gives me shit and calls me out, still steals chips off my plate when she says she isn't hungry, and she's still the person I can call at any time and complain about my mother. But now... now it's like there's this added layer to everything. I have access to *everything*.

Every happy moment and every miserable one, the way her lips and tears taste, the warmth of her hand in mine, the comfort of knowing my secrets are buried safely inside her.

She's the first person I want to talk to when I wake up and the last person on my mind when I go to sleep. Everything feels... brighter, sharper. Like the world has more colour in it or something.

I have this sense of *certainty*. I know she's with me, *really* with me, she chose me, not my money, and it's like this weight I didn't even realise I was carrying is gone. She's actually happy to be here—*with me*—it's like I won the lottery. It's not just about loving her anymore, it's about *knowing* she loves me back.

But more than all that, there's this feeling of... home. That's the best way I can describe it. When I'm with her, it doesn't matter where we are or what's going on. I *know* I'm exactly where I'm supposed to be. And that's not something I've ever felt before. I'm only eighteen, and people love to say I'm too young to know what love really is, that there's more out there to explore, but I don't need to. I've found her. The only one I'll ever need to look for.

So, yeah. Crossing that line? It's the best decision I've ever made. Because I didn't just gain a girlfriend; I gained this whole new way of seeing her, of seeing *us*. And honestly? I can't imagine going back to how it was before.

This... this is better.

This is everything.

She is everything.

Her voice splinters my thoughts. "Hey, talk to me."

"I just... I can't imagine not being with you, Hannah. Like, *ever*." The words tumble out before I start to overthink them. "I want this—us—to keep going. Even when everything else changes."

She's quiet for a beat, and my heart is in my throat. Then she smiles. "You're so cheesy."

I laugh, relieved. "You love it."

"Yeah, I do." She leans up, brushing her lips against mine in a chaste kiss. "I'll love you until the world ends."

Her words hit me harder than I expect, and if I don't say something I'll choke on my emotions. "What about after that?"

"Yes, probably even after that. Even when the robots come to get us." She sighs like I've just asked her to carry the world, as always, knowing when to follow the shift in conversation, when the moment needs a laugh instead of more tension.

I shrug, feigning nonchalance. "That's a long time you know. You might get sick of me."

"I mean... I guess that's possible. Likely even." She flops back onto my chest dramatically.

"Hey!" I grab her and pull her to me, and she giggles at my outrage. "You said till the world ends."

"And I meant it." She levels me with a look, and my heart is about to rip itself from my chest.

"You're smiling like an idiot," Hannah says, breaking into my thoughts.

"Can't help it." I pull her closer, brushing a strand of her wild hair away from her face. "I'm thinking about all the ways you've ruined me for anyone else."

She snorts. "Ruined? Please, I've upgraded you."

"Touché."

"I love you," Hannah whispers and ghosts her lips over mine.

"Until the world ends," I remind her as she tangles herself around me.

1. Back in the place I never wanted to see again

1/10/2025
Ethan

The tinted windows do nothing to shield the familiar prickle under my skin as I cross the invisible line into Valenwood. Each time I visit, it feels like the air changes around me, like the town will swallow me whole.

The big, self-important sign greets me right where the asphalt bends. *Welcome to Valenwood. Established 1901.* It's predictably what you'd expect from a small town: polished timber with carved gold lettering, surrounded by an immaculate flower bed that probably costs the council more than the library does. The thing stands there like a gatekeeper, smug and territorial, announcing to anyone passing through that Valenwood is older, cleaner, and better than whatever sad town they just crawled out of.

A few metres behind it, nailed to the a secondary post, is a smaller sign that induces an involuntary eye roll: *Voted Cleanest Town in the Country Since 1987.*

Bullshit. I'm pretty sure my grandfather bought that

title—and for some reason I'll never quite understand, he decided to plaster it everywhere. Maybe the thought of being the best at something gave him a secret thrill. After all, there's no covert 'Cleanest Town' competition, with undercover inspectors sneaking around checking for empty bins and neatly clipped lawns.

Easing my foot off the gas, I let the car coast down the hill into town, that sign disappearing behind me but the weight of it pressing square between my shoulder blades all the same. Sucking in a deep breath as I roll into the centre of town.

I haven't seen this place in almost fifteen years. Sure, I've come back for the odd Christmas or family holiday, but I would rarely leave the house. I find a spot to park and step out of the car. The spring air hits my skin, carrying a gentle warmth. I should go straight home—Mother's expecting me —but she can wait.

As I walk the familiar streets, I note that not much has changed. Sure, the edges of town have expanded so far that the outer limits are scratching the border of the next county, but that's nothing. Valenwood is still a smear on the map compared to some of the cities I've lived in and visited.

Another thing that hasn't changed is the small strip of shops that used to be the centre of town before my father built the retail monstrosity that brings in people from neighbouring towns. The mall looms over the small strip covering it in its shadow. Most of the shop owners have left and found a new home in the mall, found a new crowd to cater for that feeds their families and fills the tills, but not Fiona. Despite my father offering lower rent and prime real estate, she's retained her little bakery. Something about standing on her own two feet and not accepting charity. I like Fiona, and not only because she is one of the few people who have ever stood up to my father.

As usual, I feel like an outsider. My Armani suit perfectly tailored to my frame stands out as I reach for the door. But then it doesn't matter what I wear, I've never been seen as part of this town, just part of the family who has ruled over it for the last hundred years.

As the door to the bakery swings open, the sweet aroma of freshly baked pastries and breads hits my nose and escapes into the street. The sound of light chatter and the clinking of utensils ceases as all eyes land on me. I smile, holding my head high and rolling my shoulders back, ignoring the sudden silence and unwelcoming looks. I've always been a stranger in my own town. As I step deeper inside, I'm greeted by the enticing display of colourful treats in glass cases, and rows of perfectly baked croissants, muffins, and cakes.

Fiona appears behind the counter, and her eyes catch mine, inviting as always. "Ethan." Her smile is genuine and warm. "You're back in town?"

"Just got back." I return her smile, but we can both hear the weariness behind it.

"For how long?" I shrug, and her brows lift like a slow sunrise on her face. "The usual?"

"Yes please."

She turns her back and reaches for the coffee machine grabbing a takeaway cup. As the coffee begins to brew, the air is infused with a rich and intoxicating aroma that fills the room and I'm quietly thankful that some things never change.

Behind me, the silence has been replaced by hushed conversations and signs that everyone has returned to their meals, my presence forgotten, or ignored. I'm grateful as I take my cup and pull out my credit card.

She nudges my hand away. "On the house."

"Please—" I push it back towards her.

She smiles again and shakes her head, and I am forced to shove it back into my suit pocket, feeling suddenly chastened.

"Thanks."

"It's always good to see you, Ethan." Fiona looks like perhaps she might cross the wooden threshold between us and throw her arms around me like she used to. She doesn't. Instead, she holds my gaze for a second more before turning away and walking towards the back where her ovens keep working.

I guess some things do change.

My heart pangs a little at the thought.

I push it away and turn towards the door just as it swings open.

A woman enters the coffee shop, wearing a flowing, light-coloured summer dress that gently sways with every step. Her sun-kissed skin glows, and she smiles brightly at a threesome sitting at one of the tables near the window. Her hair is styled in loose waves that frame her face; a face I will never forget. She looks a little older, her adolescent body swallowed by feminine curves that accentuate a slender figure.

Hannah.

At the thought of her name, her eyes catch mine and my heart falters as if she'd heard me whisper it across the room. Her smile vanishes and her gaze turns cold, as she walks towards me. She doesn't acknowledge me as she heads towards the counter and waits for Fiona who appears seconds later.

"Hello, sweetheart, how are you?" Fiona beams at Hannah who smiles back.

"I'm great, how about you?"

"Oh, you know, still upright with all limbs attached." Fiona gestures at her body, showing off her hands and legs. Hannah lets out a small sound that could pass for a laugh.

"That's always good."

She winks. "I'd like to think so."

Before they can launch into a conversation about the importance of body parts, I step in, lean against the counter in her periphery, she stiffens beside me. "Hi, Hannah."

She ignores me. Fiona, thankfully, says nothing and busies herself at the coffee machine.

"Can I buy you a coffee?" I continue pretending that her ice-cold demeanour hasn't made my palms sweat and my pulse kick up.

"Not even if you were the last man on earth."

Hannah's words sting. She still hasn't turned to face me. I try a new tact. "You look good, how have you been?"

Her silence cuts through me.

A snigger rises up from somewhere in the back of the room.

I'm about to open my mouth to speak when Fiona comes back with the coffee. Her eyes snap to mine, and I think I see something like pity in them. Grinding my teeth I pretend I don't notice.

Fuck Fiona, what does she know?

Everything—every*one* in this fucking town knows everything.

"There you go, sweetie. It's so good to see you."

Hannah pulls out her wallet and Fiona takes her hands in hers. "On the house, darling."

I wonder how the hell this woman stays in business giving everything away.

"Are you sure?"

"Of course I am."

"Thank you." She beams at the older woman, and all I want is for her to look at me that way. Hell, just to look at me full stop.

Hannah turns away and heads to the table of three she greeted when she entered.

Two of them look up to stare at me, disdain colouring their features.

I know them.

Like I know everyone here.

The girl is Laura. She's dressed in black and looks like she's just walked off the set of *The Matrix*; short, cropped hair, dark glasses and a long leather jacket hanging on the back of her chair. The guy is Bruce. He was Hannah's best friend all through high school. He's always hated me, but that's because he wants to sleep with her. To her face, he denied it, but I notice the way he looks at her, the way every other guy always looked at her.

My fist tightens, the nails digging into my palm.

I give them both my best smile and raise my cup towards them.

They both look away on cue.

I guess my welcome has officially worn out.

I stare at Hannah's head for a few more seconds.

She doesn't turn around, doesn't even flinch as I cross the room and leave the coffee shop.

I stare at my phone and let it ring out. The fifth call from my mother I've let go unanswered. She can wait. I'll be back soon enough, and she'll have what she wants, what she's always wanted; me back at home and under her thumb.

Just like everyone else.

Shoving the phone back into my pocket I shake off my anger then toss my empty cup into the nearby bin keeping a lookout on the coffee shop door. When her group finally steps out, I retreat back into the shadow of the nearest building. The wall to keeps me from being spotted. I feel like a creep.

I can't help myself.

It's Hannah.

They're still talking and laughing.

My heart thunders in my chest as her face splits into a beautiful smile.

She used to smile at me all the time.

Hannah hugs Laura goodbye, and they hold onto each other in an easy embrace. When they break free Laura turns to the other man who sat with them at the table and he laces his fingers through hers as he leads her away.

Bruce hangs back. Hannah shifts her weight a little and looks at her phone before saying something. He rubs the back of his neck before stepping forward to hug her. The way she holds him is stiff, less than comfortable. He tries to linger when she releases him. Hannah brushes the awkwardness away with something funny. They both laugh and finally, she turns and walks away.

Bruce lingers watching as she puts more distance between them, turns and walks back inside the bakery.

I count to five before I start to follow her.

Hannah walks away from what's left of the once bustling strip and towards the quiet neighbourhood. It still looks like something out of a TV show. Trees line the narrowing streets. Perfectly mowed lawns. The leaves already turning green budding with flowers that will wash the street in gentle pinks and purples.

This place has always given me the creeps. It feels unnatural. Detached from the rest of the world where traffic and grime and noise fill the streets, rather than happy locals passing one another and greeting each other with smiles. Somehow, the rest of the world has moved on, but Valenwood has stood still, frozen in time.

The only changes forced upon them by a growing population and my father's plans for expansion.

I'm deep in thought almost losing Hannah as she rounds a corner.

I follow, speeding up to close the gap between us till I fall into step with her. She doesn't flinch. She isn't even surprised. Maybe my stalking wasn't as inconspicuous as I thought it was.

"Hi, Hannah."

Her only response is an eye roll before she keeps walking.

I stay in step with her as we walk in silence for almost a minute.

"You can't keep ignoring me."

I wait for a response. Turns out she can.

"I'm not going to leave you alone till you talk to me." My threat has the desired effect. She stops in her tracks to glare at me.

Hannah's eyes are beautiful brown with dancing golden flakes, and if she wasn't giving me a death stare I could easily be lost in them.

When she finally speaks, her words are laced with venom.

"What do you want?"

"I want to talk."

"That privilege is reserved for people I care about."

"Ouch." I try for humour even as I flinch like she's punched me in the gut. Her face doesn't change. I sigh. "Don't be like that, Hannah. I used to be someone you cared about."

"*Used to* being the operative words." Her hands lock across her chest and I can't help but notice how much her body has changed. Bloomed. An old desire makes its way to my cock, but I push it down.

"I can change that."

"Not if you were the last man on Earth." She says it again before spinning away from me, resuming her walk.

It's no longer casual and easy, more like a determined stiff march.

I fall back in line with her.

"I'm back for good." I try again but my words may as well be carried away by the wind. Her icy silence follows us all the way around the next corner.

It's only then that I notice we're back at her childhood house. "You still live here?" I hear the shock in my voice and instantly regret it.

Her eyes are back on me, burning with cold rage.

"We're not all rich spoiled brats who can get Mummy and Daddy to buy us an apartment in New York." Though her words are angry and laced with underlying hate, a jolt snakes its way into my body. She's been keeping track of me. "Some of us have debts to pay off and real jobs."

"Hannah..." I try to reach for her, but she flinches away from my touch as if I'm about to strike her then makes her way up the three stairs to the front door. She doesn't look at me as she fishes her keys from her bag and stabs one into the keyhole. "Can I see you again?"

Hannah slams the door shut, and I'm left alone in the street.

My phone vibrates in my pocket, and I pull it out.

It's my mother.

Again.

As I turn back in the direction of home, I realise Hannah didn't say no.

I let the thought keep me company all the way home.

2. The prodigal son

1/10/2025
Ethan

"The prodigal son returns." She is sitting in the sunroom, perfectly made up, her large sunglasses sitting heavily across her thickly made-up face. She is trying to pretend that age hasn't caught up with her. The plastic surgeon can only hide so much.

"Mother." I bend down to kiss her cheek, mostly so that she doesn't see my eye roll.

"You've been ignoring my calls."

"I've been busy."

"Doing what?"

"Reacquainting myself with the town."

"Why would you do that?"

I ignore the question and sit down. Martha, one of the loveliest women I have even known and my mother's personal assistant, rushes into the room. I think my mother just reinvented the term 'overworked, underpaid maid.'

"Can I get you a cup of coffee, Mr Valen?"

I hate that she calls me that.

"Ethan, and no, I can get one myself in a moment thanks, Martha."

She looks at me uncomfortably.

"Don't be stupid, just get him a coffee, the way his dad likes it."

Martha gives a quick acknowledgment and flees the room.

"I can make my own coffee, Mother."

"Yes, but you don't *need* to, that's why we have people."

"I don't need people; I'm a perfectly capable adult."

"As you've demonstrated on multiple occasions," she bites, likely referring to the numerous *incidents* my parents have had to bail me out of due to some stupid decisions on my part. "Just because you've been living as an independent, there's no need to be selfish. Martha needs this job to look after her children; if you did everything in her stead how will she pay her bills?"

My jaw tightens, a pulse of heat running up my neck, I have no desire to get into this argument with my mother. She always got her way, one way or another; trying anything else is just delaying the inevitable. I let it go as Martha walks into the room with my cup and sets it on the table already adorned with a tray of biscuits, cheese and finger sandwiches.

She looks at my mother who blatantly dismisses her with a wave of the hand and the undertow of rage that always accompanies me when she is in a room, flares inside my stomach. I know we are privileged, but it's no excuse to treat people like shit.

"We need to talk business."

I blow out a long breath. "Not right now."

"Don't you dare sigh at me as if you're carrying the

world on your shoulders. You've been dodging me and your responsibilities all week.'

"I haven't been dodging my responsibilities."

"I'm already under enough stress after your dad..."

"You don't need to keep bringing that up. The board is looking after everything. Maybe we just need a few extra days to come to terms with...you know..."

Her dismissive huff cuts deep, slicing the thin veil of patience I wore for this interaction. "You've never been responsible, not since you were a kid and ran around with that little gold digger."

"Don't talk about Hannah like that." Heat envelopes my face and burns my insides.

"Well, if it wasn't her it was someone else, you sure have been through a number of them, haven't you?"

"Them?"

"Girls."

"Mother..."

She continues as if I haven't spoken, "but now you're thirty-five it's time to settle down with someone on your level and get on with it."

"My level?"

"Yes, your wealth, education, social status, I would say your intelligence, but I question that."

I don't respond as anger threatens to erupt. She takes my silence as agreement.

"I've organised dinner with the Greene's. You remember Miranda? She's still single. Of course, to look at her you'd know why but that's no matter."

My mouth falls open at my mother's audacity. Miranda Greene, known to her friends as Sookie, has always been on the heavier side, and perhaps a little too pale for my liking, but from our interactions over the years, she also seems fiercely intelligent, funny as hell and openly living with her partner as a full-blown happy lesbian.

"She comes from old money, like we do; it would be a good match. You can have a spring wedding and have an heir running around by late next year."

"I'm not marrying Miranda Greene."

"Why not?"

"Because we don't love each other." I decide to leave Miranda's sexual preferences out of this conversation. My mother is wicked enough and I refuse to give her any more ammunition to hurt anyone.

"Pfffttt, love is overrated. You can keep a few of your girls on the side for *funsies*. Marriage is a business deal. Love is for the poor."

"Jesus, Mum."

"Oh, grow up! You've been a child long enough. Dinner is on Friday at 7pm sharp, and you better be on your best behaviour." She gives me a sharp, harsh look, her eyes fixed on me.

"Fine," I grumble and take a sip of my too-strong coffee to drown out the rest of the words threatening to spill out of my mouth. I twist my mouth at the drink, wondering if that's why my father's entire life tasted like bitterness and disappointment.

3. It's not stalking if they know you're there

The alarm screams at me. I roll over in my warm sheets and my hand fumbles across the nightstand where I grab my phone and silence it. Just past seven. Early enough that half the town's still tucked in, but late enough I should be getting ready for work.

Groaning, I shove the covers back, and swing my legs over the edge of the bed. The floor is cold against my feet. Everything in this town is always cold—predictable, polished, and utterly lifeless. I dig through the laundry pile and pull out a clean-enough shirt, yanking it over my head as I shuffle toward the mirror.

This is the kind of town where the lights go out early and everyone seems to be tucked in by ten. Nothing ever happens here. That's why my parents moved us here. That's why everyone stays.

There's no crime, no drugs, no surprises. Just safety. Stillness. Routine.

Until there was Ethan. A shock to the system. A hurricane in a town built of straw. He was the one unexpected thing that ever happened to me here. And now, he's back.

The audacity of it makes my skin itch. In fact, everything about his family makes me queasy.

I twist my hair into a ponytail and start brushing my teeth a little too vigorously. There's a reason I've spent the last two years taking extra classes after hours, saving every penny, so I can get out of dodge. I have just one more month till the semester ends, then I can leave this shithole that holds far too many memories, move to London and try and make a better life for myself. See what's out there and see more of the world. I cannot stand being in such a tiny place with so little to offer. There's no place for growth, there is nothing here, nothing other than a slow, sad death.

Well death or a certain future working for the Vales which is basically the same thing. A family so rich this town is named after them, Valenwood. God how I hate it here.

Bending over the sink, I rinse and spit, staring at my reflection. "Urgh." I scowl at myself and walk away. How is he ruining my morning already?

I hate living under their shadow, that they feel like they own all of us, and that we all owe them some kind of debt of gratitude for keeping the town above water during the pandemic. While every other town suffered with food and medicine shortages, with their money keeping our town going, we managed to stay afloat, unperturbed by the troubles of the outside world. We were in our own little bubble of safety.

Of course we were grateful to the Vales, but even after all this time it feels as though they lord it over our heads, and we are their fateful obedient puppets here to do their bidding.

They got the support of the town to stick the monstrosity of a mall on the outskirts, effectively sucking the life blood from the lively town centre that once thrived. Now it's only the locals keeping the small business afloat. The ones that refused to conform.

They make my blood boil. Just because they have money doesn't mean they're better than us, yet everybody grovels when Mr. Vale comes prancing through town.

Thank you, Mr. Vale. Thank you, Mrs. Vale, you are so kind. We love you, we worship you.

Well fuck that. They will never see me on my knees! Not like Mum and Dad. Yes, the pandemic hit Dad's business hard, yes, he had to be bailed out, and yes, we only kept the house because of the handout Mr Vale was willing to give us. But it crushed a piece of my dad's soul, and I hate that he stole my stoic happy father from me by turning him into another soulless slave in the Vale empire.

I slap on some mascara and swipe gloss across my lips, the rage bubbling just beneath my skin.

"Stop it," I whisper to myself and push away from my reflection. But I can't stop it, the creeping thoughts, the utter annoyance. He's back. Waltzing into Fiona's and offering to buy me a coffee, like nothing ever happened, like the slate is perfectly clean.

In the kitchen, the Post-it note on the fridge declares that Mum has made my lunch. Again. That woman is a saint. I snatch the sandwich and salad container from inside, shutting the door a little too hard. The jam bottles jingle in protest. I look at the white machine apologetically.

At least I'll have the house to myself soon. Not that I mind living with them. In fact, I enjoy it, most of the time, when I don't hate being thirty-five and single. They're off to France for their thirtieth wedding anniversary. That's something to celebrate, loving somebody that much for that long. I love that it's such a rare thing that they're still together. I love the way that my dad looks at my mum like he really sees her. I love the way that they fight for each other because there is passion there, and neither of them have lost the will to fight for what they have.

I love my parents. I just don't love where we live, and I don't love the choices they've made for me, but I love them for allowing me to finally leave and make my own way in the world.

I've done everything they've asked, and I'm going to go make it on my own, on my terms, away from here, and finally, finally away from *him* and his family.

Because, of course, he's back.

I heard about his father. Everyone has. He's a Vale.

That same pang I felt when I first heard pulsates inside me—the pull to pick up the phone and call him, ask him if he is okay, knowing he wouldn't be. But I push the feeling down—deep, deep down—until it evaporates.

As I pack my lunch away, the knock comes.

I know who it is. Taste it in the back of my throat like a warning. I shouldn't open the door, I shouldn't even look at it, but a part of me is stupidly curious while the other part just wants to hurt him. I can't do that through a closed door.

And there he is.

Ethan Vale.

Like a ghost who forgot he was supposed to stay dead.

He's taller. Broader. The same tousled hair and perfect face I used to kiss in the dark. He looks older. Like the years made him sharper, somehow, more solid. But his eyes—they're exactly the same. Big. Blue. Unapologetic.

A tremble of discomfort spreads up my spine and my heartbeat kicks up.

He holds out a bouquet—white lilies and yellow tulips. My favourites. Once.

"Ethan," I manage to say flatly despite the storm inside.

"Morning, Hannah. These are for—"

Before he can finish whatever little speech he'd prepared, the familiar rattle of Mrs. Jenkins' garden gate breaks the moment. She appears a few metres away, tugging at her sunhat and squinting through her thick lenses.

Without hesitation I snatch the bouquet from his hands and march past him, forgoing the sheer joy at seeing his shocked expression.

"Mrs. Jenkins! These are for you."

She stops in her tracks, blinking behind thick glasses. Her expression warms and she steps closer. "For *me*? What's all this about?"

My lips tug into a slow grin. "Because I can and because you deserve it."

She beams and totters over with a hand over her heart. "You're such a darling. Harold used to bring me flowers, you know. Before his knees gave out and he got lazy." Her chuckle is dry as she winks at me.

A broad grin splits my face as I pass it to her. "You deserve every petal."

She glances at Ethan. "Is this your young man, dear?"

I laugh. "God, no. Just a door-to-door florist."

Mrs. Jenkins chuckles. "Well, aren't you handsome! You should come by more often, brighten the place up."

He gives her that sheepish smile I used to love. She melts a little.

"You Remind me a little of that Ethan Vale." She squints trying for a better look.

"I get that a lot." His smile broadens and he winks at her, sending red through her cheeks.

I huff.

"You two—?"

"Oh, no," I cut in, laughing sharp and dry. "He's just leaving."

"That's a pity." the old woman wobbles her eyebrows at me.

"Not really." I shrug, the lie hanging quietly between us.

Mrs. Jenkins tilts her head toward the door, lips pressed into a knowing smile. "I'd invite you in for a coffee, sweetheart, but I'm guessing you've got work."

"Yeah, I should get going," I steer her toward her gate. "Rain check, okay?"

"Absolutely." Something tender flickers across her face. Clutching the bouquet to her chest, she disappears behind her gate.

I turn on my heel, march past Ethan, still standing at the threshold, back inside, and shut the door behind me.

Not gently.

The slam echoes in the quiet. My forehead rests against the door, breath ragged.

He looks good. Too good. Like someone who belonged in a different story, a different life. A version of mine that never existed. His face has matured—sharper jawline, more confidence—but his eyes haven't changed. Neither has the way they undo me.

My pulse drums against my ribs. My cheeks burn.

I slide to the floor, heart racing, forehead pressed to the wood.

God help me.

Ethan Vale is back in Valenwood.

And I am not ready for what that could mean.

5/10/25 - Tuesday
Hannah

I'm jamming my feet into my shoes when the knock comes.

Right on time.

Laura never runs late. She's the only person I know who can be five minutes early and still apologise for not arriving earlier.

Zipping up my jacket, I open the door.

There she is. Insulated in an all-black outfit that clings to her like armour, dark sunglasses perched on her head and her long black coat sweeping around her calves. She looks intimidating, sharp and sleek, but that's only on the outside; the show she puts up to the rest of the world. I'm lucky enough to know better. Laura is the gentlest and most caring person I know.

Laura's not just my best friend—she's the sister I never had. She's been there through everything: my mum's illness, that awful year our dog died, every heartbreak I've barely survived. She's never once let me down. Never lied to me. She's steady. Solid. The kind of person who never disappears when things get hard, who brings soup unasked when you're feeling down, and makes fun of you when you've embarrassed yourself and never lets you live it down, who gives you a hug when you're crying and asks what you need rather than tell you how to feel. She's selfless, sweet, and someone else has finally seen it too and will soon be stealing her away from me.

Or so he thinks.

She stands at my door beaming like always.

We made plans—something wedding-related. Maybe

checking out sample dresses for her reception look, or maybe scouting table runners. I don't remember. Honestly, it doesn't matter. If she asked me to wrestle a bear while wearing heels, I'd be there in a heartbeat.

"Ready?" she's holding up a takeaway coffee because she knows I can't human without it.

The coffee scent calls me like a beacon, and I step outside, locking the door behind me.

The spring air is crisp but not cold, the kind that smells like freshly cut grass and the faint sweetness of the blooming wisteria trees peppered around town. The sun peeks out over the few clouds in the sky and promises to push away the cold while the town wakes up at its own pace.

We walk in step, sipping coffee and laughing about something dumb Sam said. Laura loops her arm through mine and leans her head against my shoulder.

"Still can't believe it's actually happening," she glances at her ring. "It still feels weird on my finger. Like it's too good to be true."

"It's perfect. You're perfect. And Sam's obsessed with you. He's stuck with us now." I giggle, nudging her shoulder.

"He's very excited to be part of a threesome."

"Is he aware that he's the third wheel?"

"Pretty sure he's gotten the hint over the last five years."

"I guess he has put up with our shit."

"The man has had no choice. He knows we're a package deal. Plus, he lives in hope that one day we'll actually get together."

"Maybe we should, just to fuck with the guy... shower scene?"

We burst into laughter. "We'll break him."

"I'd be okay with that," I wipe my eyes.

"But I like this one. A lot." Her voice softens.

I let out a mock groan. "Yes, I know, okay. No shower then."

"Actually, I think that would devastate him more."

We laugh, loud and unfiltered, drawing curious glances. I picture Sam's face—equal parts betrayed and confused.

"Damnit, He really is a good one, isn't he?"

"The best." She's all smiles and rosy cheeks.

We round the corner, and something about the shift in light casts the street in a gentle haze—spring flowers spilling out of planters, the scent of jasmine somewhere on the breeze, shopfronts glinting with sun. It's perfect in that quiet, small-town way I always claim to hate.

"I just can't wait to see you walk down that aisle," I bump her shoulder. "I'll try not to cry all over your train."

"You better cry! It's practically a rule. And hey, maybe if you stand next to me looking all teary-eyed and pathetic, some poor guy will finally wife you up too."

"I'm perfectly happy being single and pathetic. Especially if my options are 'some poor guy'."

Laura grins. "What about Bruce? That man would crawl on broken glass if you so much as hinted—"

"Oh my God, just don't! Please." I cringe so hard I think my teeth will fall out. "The man still doesn't understand the concept of the friend zone. He's like a lost little puppy who thinks every belly rub is a marriage proposal."

Laura cackles. "Wait—what? You rubbed his belly?"

"It was *one* time, and it's not what you think."

"It's always what I think. And Bruce definitely took that as a cosmic signal you were soulmates."

"Oh God, he probably did. I'm done for." My hand grips hers, desperately and I squeeze, looking directly into her eyes. "The man would probably propose at Fiona's using a donut as a ring and want our engagement party at the local."

"Oh babe, I'm excited for you. It's going to be sooooo romantic."

I push off her in mock disgust. "I'm not *that* desperate."

"But aren't you? Really???"

We're both in hysterics, my ribs hurt. She's wiping her eyes, and I'm halfway through trying to catch my breath when footsteps fall behind us. Slow. Measured.

Then a voice, too close to mistake.

"Or you could always consider a better option than Bruce—say, me."

My laughter dies in my throat. I freeze.

Ethan Vale.

He's right behind us. His voice slithers into my spine and sets every nerve on edge. My heart rockets into my throat. My whole body coils tight.

Laura's the first to move. She turns, eyes narrowing, and plants her hand flat against his chest like she's keeping back a tide.

"She's definitely not *that* desperate, creep."

"Yet..." He tries for a joke, but that's like trying to save a sinking ship with a teacup.

"Jesus, Ethan," she snaps. "Can you take a hint? Nobody wants you here."

I don't look at him. I can't. My skin is buzzing and my mouth has gone dry. Of all the moments. Of all the places. How long had he been following us?

"Five minutes, Hannah," he says, voice quieter now. "Just talk to me."

Laura doesn't even flinch. "You've already ruined her day with one! Just go away. She doesn't need saving, or your half-baked apologies, or whatever sad-boy speech you've rehearsed."

She grabs my arm again, and I let her. I let her steer me away, because my legs won't move on their own. My pulse thuds too loud in my ears.

I don't look back. I won't.

But I feel his eyes burning into my spine.

Laura cracks a joke about Bruce, and I force a laugh, but it sounds strangled and hollow. She squeezes my arm as we keep moving forward.

What the hell is he doing here?

Why won't he just stay gone?

And why the hell does my heart still claw at my ribs like it'll break clean through if I don't turn around and look at him—just once?

6/10/25 - Wednesday
Ethan

The air con spews out cool air and my hands curl around the steering wheel as I sit pretending I am not a complete idiot. The last few days attempting to reach Hannah have been a disaster. The flowers bombed. Laura played shield maiden like Hannah was a celebrity dodging paparazzi.

A spike of electricity surges up my spine as I spot her walking down Main, tote bag over her shoulder, hair tied up, oblivious to the chaos she's leaving in her wake— because I am the chaos, or worse, maybe she's completely aware and just doesn't care.

Inhaling, I brush away the thought.

I get out of the car as Hannah heads into the bakery. I'm about to cross the street when headlights blind me and the unmistakable grumble of Frank's beat-up truck swerves into my path. The thing screeches to a halt, blocking my way.

Perfect.

Frank's at the wheel, Rob riding shotgun, and Barry leaning half out the window like he's got nothing better to do than play small-town security.

"Morning, Vale," Barry calls, chewing a toothpick. "Funny seeing you here."

"Hilarious." I take a step forward, attempting to round the car when Frank, eases his foot off the brake just enough to inch forward and block me again.

"Move the truck." My jaw tightens.

Rob gives a slow, smug shrug. "Can't. Frank's gotta recalibrate the GPS. Town's tricky to navigate, you know. Real easy to get turned around."

"Seriously?"

Frank waves from the cab. "Yeah, wouldn't want anyone getting lost."

"Can't get lost getting a coffee."

"You'd be surprised," Barry chimes in.

Tension climbs from my jaw into my skull and my fists clench tightly at my sides. Everything I try, she dodges. Every inch forward, someone's there to shove me back.

"You three always run interference? Or is this a special subscription package for me?"

Barry shrugs. "Interference? We're just trying to fix what's broken."

"Me too," I whisper too low for them to hear as my gaze flicks past the bonnet—I catch a glimpse of Hannah as she turns the corner.

The engine rumbles, but they don't move. The truck lingers long enough to make the message clear.

"Look at that, looks like I got it working again," Frank chimes.

"You're a damn hero," I offer him.

"You're right, I should get a medal."

By the time they finally pull away, Hannah's long gone, and I'm standing there on the curb, furious and humiliated, with three local heroes doing their part to keep me out of her orbit.

I let out a harsh breath, turn and make my way back to my car.

Tomorrow.

I'll try again tomorrow.

7/10/25 - Thursday
Ethan

The school bell rings, and kids pour out in small chaotic clusters. Backpacks bouncing, laughter echoing like tiny explosions.

Scanning the crowd, heel tapping against the front of my car seat.

And there she is.

Ponytail swaying, clipboard in hand, that same genuine smile she reserves for parents she doesn't hate. Her glance skims the street—a practiced move—something protective and innate. Once, then again. On the third sweep it lands on me. I flash some teeth, raise my hand and wave. Her eyes narrow.

Hannah doesn't wave back, doesn't smile. She grabs her phone, dials and speaks briefly, before tucking it away and turning her attention back to the parent she was speaking to.

Two minutes later, sirens.

Two patrol cars screech in like they're responding to a hostage situation. One blocks my front bumper. The other swings tight behind. I can't move my car even if I wanted to.

I raise my hands slowly as the first cop approaches. He looks about twelve. Fresh face, uniform crisp like it's straight from the package.

The window lowers with a muted whir and I lean out slightly, "What's up, Matchsticks?"

The red-haired skinny cop twitches at the name. "It's Officer Burns now." He steps closer to the car.

"What's this all about?"

"Please step out of the vehicle. Hands where I can see them." His voice cracks slightly as he takes another step.

I draw a calming breath through my nose and pop the door. "You serious right now, Matchsticks?"

This guy was still a kid when I left this town. His dad works for mine, just like everyone else here.

He swallows. "Please call me Officer Burns. We received a complaint. Watching children. Suspicious behaviour."

"You've got to be kidding."

"Well... you're loitering, if nothing else..."

"Loitering?" My shoulders tense.

Sheriff Derry walks into my periphery. The man has been keeping this town calm since the cassette era. More babysitter with a badge than cop, which works just fine in a place where nothing ever happens. "Get in the car, Ethan."

"Walt..."

"Just go with the kid so we can clear this up." He looks at me with his blue paternal eyes, and I shrug.

"Please turn around," Matchsticks mumbles, and I do as he says.

The cuffs close around my wrists. Gently. Like he's scared I might shatter. When he guides me to the back of the car, he holds the door open like a valet. I slide in without a word.

Behind the school fence, the crowd gathers, a river of faces. Kids' eyes stretch wide, parents raise phones like they're at a concert, women whisper behind their hands. Their gazes press into my back, every one of my moves scrutinised, memorised ready to fuel the rumours that will ripple through town over shared coffees and park walks. I spot Hannah, calm as anything, looking on with a satisfied expression.

The twitch at the corner of my mouth almost betrays my disbelief.

The cell is tiny and reeks of bleach and something sour; I'd rather not think about what it could be. They don't even pretend to take this 'arrest' seriously. I'm not booked. Not cautioned. The door isn't even locked, I could walk out of here at any time. I'm basically a kid in detention waiting for his parents to pick him up.

I pace the tiny room, shoes scuffing tile, oscillating between mild fury and something resembling admiration.

She played me.

I can't believe she called the cops on me.

Hannah has gone too far.

So what if I was sitting like a stalker outside the primary school she works at waiting to pounce on her when she finished her day? I just wanted a conversation. I wasn't perving. Of course *she* knows that. She knows because she's blocked every burner phone number I've used, shut the door to her house multiple times, and has had all her friends do it too. Her mother was at least slightly apologetic as she asked me to go away. I'm starting to think she really means it when she says she doesn't want to speak to me.

My phone buzzes in my jacket pocket and I reach for it, the incessant ringtone screeching in the small station.

Matchsticks appear in front of me.

He shifts his weight, barely looking at me. "You're not allowed phones."

"Trust me when I say I don't want this call either, but one of us will have to pick up."

I show him the screen. The word 'Mother' flashes across it.

Matchstick's face turns a deeper shade of red.

I push the phone through the bars towards him. "Would

you like to answer and explain to my mother why her only son is currently sitting in a holding cell?"

He swallows, then thrusts it toward me like it's radioactive and backs up a full step.

"Mother," I answer, dragging a hand down my face.

Matchsticks disappears around a corner.

"What the hell is going on?" she snaps before I can say another word. "I've just had a call from Walt Derry. Something about you being *arrested*? Again?"

"I wasn't arrested," I mutter. "Just detained. Briefly."

"For what, Ethan?"

I close my eyes. "Loitering near a school."

"Oh *goody*, loitering. Here I was thinking it was something to do with a woman... again."

"Well... it kind of was. I was trying to talk to Hannah."

There's a silence so sharp I swear I hear her blinking. "The little teacher girl?"

"Moth—"

"Are you an idiot? Why are you revisiting that when I've organised dinner with Greene's tomorrow night? I've told you Miranda will be there."

"And I've told you—"

"I don't want to hear it! She's clearly not interested. The girl understands her place and it's time you do too."

"Thanks for the support." Arguing is futile.

"Oh don't be so bloody dramatic. Look—" I hear her moving through the house, opening a drawer. "I'll call whoever I need to call and smooth this over. But for God's sake, Ethan, *stop making a scene*. You've been back a week and the entire town's already talking. This is not the time for another scandal. Not with your father and all."

I rub the back of my neck squeezing my eyes shut. "Yeah okay. Sure."

"And tomorrow night. You will *not* be late."

I let my head fall back against the cell wall. "Yup. Looking forward to it."

She hangs up.

I tuck the phone into my pocket when Matchsticks comes around the corner. He is holding a tray with a cup of coffee and some muffins. I open the door for him, and he walks into my cell placing the tray down.

He looks embarrassed as I look at the offering.

"It's all we have, but my aunt baked the muffins."

I pick one off the plate and shove some into my mouth. I've definitely had worse, but not by much. "Tell her they are delicious."

He beams and is about to add something else when Sheriff Derry waltzes around the corner.

"Mr. Vale," he says, trying and failing to sound official. "You're free to go. No charges filed."

"No kidding?" I mutter.

"Misunderstanding. Ms. Jones was... concerned. It's been logged and dismissed."

"Thanks for the hospitality."

Matchsticks flushes deeper as I walk around him and towards the corridor letting myself out of the tiny station.

She sent the cops.

I should be furious.

Instead, I'm impressed.

I climb into my car and scrub a hand over my face, the spring night air hits my face like a slap. Maybe it's the slap I needed to wake up.

4. The day the world ended, and I got stuck with this loser

01/11/2025
Hannah

Jerking up in my bed, I prick my ears to listen. A window breaks somewhere in the distance, a scream cuts through it. The more the world tilts back into reality and out of the dream I was having, the more I listen to what should be silence but it's not. The world is alive and it shouldn't be. Because it's pitch-black outside and this is Valenwood.

I tune into the sound. I swear I hear a gunshot, which is impossible. It has to be my heart thundering in my chest, because why would anybody be shooting anything in the middle of the night?

There's another scream and a growl, and maybe another broken window.

I have no idea what's going on.

Crashing downstairs pulls me from my reverie. My breath catches, sweat creeping down my neck, ears straining to hear more.

Another crash.

Something heavy hitting the floor.

My stomach knots.

I push back the covers and slide out of bed, my pulse a frantic drum in my ears. My mind scrambles for a logical explanation. A window left open? An animal that got inside? Maybe Laura forgot something last night and came back to grab it?

But deep down, I know better. Someone is inside. A small part of me, the five-year-old girl part suddenly wishes my parents were home instead of an ocean away.

The floor is cold under my feet. Stepping lightly, I creep toward the stairs. I descend, hands gripping the railing, my knuckles white under the moonlight.

Another crash, closer this time.

My stomach twists, but I push forward.

When I turn the corner at the bottom of the stairs—I freeze.

There's a man in my house.

I strain against the darkness and look at the figure.

His back is hunched, his shoulders heaving, and he's dragging something off the counter, sending dishes shattering to the floor. His clothes are torn and stained, his head tilted at a strange angle as he groans low and guttural.

I recognise the figure, all the darkness in the world can't disguise his sheer size and large eagle tattoo on the back of his neck. "Frank?"

He jerks around at the sound of my voice.

My blood turns to ice.

His skin is ashen, his lips peeled back in something that isn't quite a snarl but isn't quite human either. His eyes are sunken and cloudy, and when he sees me, he lets out a wet, gurgling sound.

This isn't Frank, it's a strange, demented version of the kindest gentlest man I know.

"What are you doing here, Frank?" My quivering voice is barely a whisper.

He stares at me with a blank look, then he lunges.

A scream claws up my throat, but I barely manage to stumble back before the weight of another body slams into him from the side. They hit the ground hard, grunts and snarls filling the air, and I press myself against the wall, adrenalin flooding my body.

Ethan.

He wrestles the thing to the ground, heaving in ragged bursts as he pins it down. "Hannah—" he grits out, eyes flicking to mine. "We have to go. *Now.*"

I stand frozen, chest rising and falling too fast. This isn't happening. It *can't* be happening.

The thing beneath him thrashes, its fingers clawing at the tiles, letting out a sound that makes my skin crawl.

Ethan lands a devasting blow, the hard crack fracturing reverberating through the room. A low groan spills from Frank and he remains motionless on the ground.

Ethan doesn't wait for me to move. He gets off in a swift motion, grabbing my wrist and yanks me forward, his grasp firm and unrelenting.

"Come on," he jerks his chin toward the door, urging me toward the door. "*Now, Hannah!*"

I barely manage to keep up as he pulls me towards the windows. He parts the curtain just a fraction so we can peek outside.

There are people milling around the streets, but they're not milling so much as dragging their bodies around, groaning. Car alarms are going off in the distance, dogs are howling. I have no idea what the fuck is going on.

Blood dribbles down the faces of a few. Their clothes are torn and they're all in their pyjamas, hair dishevelled, looking like they've just woken up from sleep, except none of them are awake. They're all sleepwalking like zombies. I push away from the window, and my heart drops to the pit of my stomach, where it just keeps, falling and falling and falling.

"Ethan, what the fuck is going on?"

"I don't know, Hannah. I don't know. But we have to go." His voice is laced with panic as his head swivels behind us to where Frank lies moaning. "All I know is that we aren't safe and we have to go now!"

Even as he speaks a window smashes somewhere in the back, followed by a disturbed growl. Someone is coming into the house and that someone doesn't sound human. I can't even believe I'm thinking these thoughts because even as I'm thinking them, they don't compute. My mind can't make sense of what's going on.

Ethan grabs my wrist and pulls me towards the door. "We gotta get out of here."

"Where are we going?" I half-pull away from his grip.

"We have to make it to the mall for now. That's the only place we're gonna be safe."

"How the hell do you expect us to—"

"Hannah, don't argue with me, just come on!" His voice is clipped and there's fear there. It mirrors my own, except while I'm falling apart, he's keeping himself together so he can get us both to safety.

He cracks the door open, and we look towards the street. It looks eerily deserted, but we both know that it's not. Somewhere out there imminent danger is lurking, waiting to spring out from the darkness.

The cold catches me by surprise. It's still spring—the

days are warm, but the nights are sharp, and I hadn't realised how cosy it was indoors until now. The air burns my throat as Ethan pulls me forward, his hand anchored on my wrist.

A sudden noise makes me jerk and I look to my left. Mrs. Jenkins is standing under her door light in her nightgown with a strange look on her face. She's pale and sweaty and her eyes are glazed over.

"Mrs. Jenkins, are you all right?" I want to take a step towards her, but Ethan's hand clamps down.

"Don't," he whispers, and I take a harder look at her. Her nightgown is covered in blood.

"Mrs. Jenkins—" but she doesn't let me finish. She bares her teeth and reaches out as she lunges at us. Ethan pulls my wrist and we scramble into the street, running into the night, her screams and snarls chasing us into the darkness.

The streets are alive in the worst possible way.

Groans echo in the darkness, glass shatters somewhere in the distance, a dog howls, and there's a scream—cut short. We stay off the main roads, darting through the shadows, but even here, they're everywhere. Shuffling figures, too slow to be human, too real to be anything else.

My mind can't grapple with this reality. I can't wrap my head around it.

My lungs burn, breath coming in ragged gasps, it curls in the cold air.

Ethan comes to a sudden stops, pulling me to a halt. The air saws in and out of him, harsh and audible in the quiet, but his eyes are locked ahead, frozen.

I follow his gaze—and my stomach drops.

There's a man standing under the dark streetlight.

I know him. I know everyone in this town. *Rob Thompson.* We were in the same class. We may have even shared a few secret kisses once. He's happily married now with two kids. Married to little miss perfect Emma Thompson. She made my life a living hell in high school. A strange, misplaced jealousy flickers. I don't think it's much to do with the fact she snagged Rob, but about the life they have, the kind of life I thought *I'd* have. But I was never made for this town. I was always made for bigger things.

"Rob?" I whisper, stepping forward before Ethan's fingers tightens on me.

"Shh." His warning is low, urgent.

Rob doesn't move. His eyes are locked on us, but there's nothing behind them, no flicker of recognition. His shirt is missing, his broad frame exposed to the cold, pyjama pants hanging low on his hips.

"Back up. Nice and slow," Ethan murmurs, stepping back and pushing me behind him.

Rob follows. One step forward, another, mirroring us like a predator stalking prey.

"Rob, it's *us*," I say, trying again. "Snap out of it."

Ethan shushes me harder, but I've never been one to do what he tells me.

"Don't you tell me to shut up!" I snap. "Rob, come on, man—"

A voice calls out behind us. "Hannah?"

I whip around. *Laura.*

She's standing a little way down the street, wide-eyed, clutching a makeshift weapon—some kind of pipe or bat, held tight in both hands. Relief crashes over me for a split-second before it curdles into terror.

Because Rob moves.

Faster than he should be able to, faster than any of us expect. He makes a beeline for Laura before lunging at her.

Laura screams as he slams into her, knocking her to

the lush green lawn. The pipe clatters out of her hands, rolling away into the dark. I move without thinking, but Ethan's already grabbing me, yanking me in the opposite direction.

"No!" I shriek, twisting against his hold. "We have to—"

"We *can't*." His voice is sharp, edged with something I don't want to name. *Something like knowing.*

Laura is still struggling, screaming, but Rob is on her, pinning her down. And then—

She lets out a high-pitched, ragged scream that stabs straight through my ribs, leaving a ringing emptiness behind. My stomach twists, my hands clench, and I stumble back as if the sound has physical weight. Somewhere in the pitch and terror of it is the awful understanding that she's not getting back up.

Oxygen burns in my throat, the air refusing to reach my lungs.

Ethan doesn't let me stop. He pulls me harder, forcing us onward, and then we're running.

The streets blur past as my feet pound he ground, shadows stretching and folding over themselves. We keep going, ears straining for the slightest sound, trying to outrun them.

We duck into a row of bushes, crouching low, holding our breath as figures shuffle past. People I *know*. People I used to wave to in the grocery store, people who used to smile at me in passing. Now, they groan and drag their feet, heads twitching at odd angles, moving in ways no human should.

This isn't real.

It *can't* be real.

But my eyes don't lie.

We wait in the dark until the street is empty again.

Then, Ethan turns to me, voice low and urgent. "We have to get to the mall."

My next breath shudders out of me. "No, we *can't*—"

"It's our best chance," he cuts in. "It has supplies. Shelter. We can block the entrances—"

"What? No," I hiss, thinking of the mall, an alluring bright beacon of lights. "That's the worst place to be. A giant glass box, with nowhere to run. We'll be trapped inside."

"And they will be trapped outside!" His panic is starting to wane, shifting gear into exasperation. "Hannah, haven't you watched any zombie movies?"

"But—"

"My family owns the place. We'll have access to everything. That's an advantage. And we don't have time to argue."

Somewhere behind us, someone screams. The sound is guttural, awful, and cuts off too soon.

"We don't have time for this shit. Let's go." Ethan doesn't give me another chance to protest. He grabs my wrist again, and we run.

We don't stop until the mall looms ahead of us, a hulking shadow against the night sky. All the power is out. The only lights are the eerie glow of emergency exit signs, casting red and green reflections like watching eyes. The glass storefronts are black, offering no glimpse inside, just distorted reflections of the street behind us.

I yank my hand out of Ethan's grasp. "This is a mistake."

He doesn't even hesitate. "We don't have a choice."

A groan echoes from somewhere behind us.

Then another.

And then—

A horde rounds the corner.

Shapes flood the street, moving as one, their collective shuffling rising into a deafening sound. The closest one lets out a strangled wail, snapping its head in our direction.

Ethan grabs my wrist. "Run!"

We sprint toward a side entrance, my pulse roaring in my ears. The horde is behind us, loud and volatile.

My grip tightens in his shirt. "Hurry up, hurry up." My voice, high pitched and sputtering.

"I'm trying." Ethan punches in the code with trembling fingers, the steel security door clicking open just as the first of them reach the edge of the parking lot.

We shove ourselves inside, throwing our weight against the heavy door, slamming it shut. Ethan locks it, fingers slamming numbers into the keypad.

For a moment, there's only silence, just our uneven gasps in the dark.

Then—

A bang.

Faint, but insistent.

Another follows.

Then another.

Seconds later fists hammer the metallic structure sending echoes down the long concrete corridor.

The zombies are outside.

We press ourselves against the cool metal, listening to the sound of the undead trying to get in.

For now, the door holds.

For now, we're safe.

But we're also trapped.

5. This Can't be happening

Hannah is panting, her face flushed, a light sheen of sweat covering her forehead. She clutches her head in her hands, repeating, "This can't be happening." Her voice rises in panic. "What the hell is happening, Ethan? This can't be happening."

I try to break through the rising wall of panic around her. "I've got you, you're safe, we're here, you're safe."

"Safe from what?" she spits, still frantic. "What the hell is going on?"

I grip her arms, my gaze catching hers. "I don't know. All I know is I woke up in the middle of the night, and somebody was trying to eat me."

Her mouth drops open, like I'm crazy, like she hasn't just witnessed the same thing with her own eyes, but I keep talking, trying to calm her. Deep down, she knows what she saw and knows what I'm saying is the truth.

"How did you get to my house?"

"I don't know but I have you now," I try to reassure her. "You're safe. We're here."

I try to pull her into my arms, but she pulls away. "Don't fucking touch me. I hate you."

"Hannah, we've got bigger problems right now."

"I know, but you don't get to touch me. The fact that the world is ending around us doesn't change that I'd rather be dead than stuck here with you."

"Wow, that's a great way to thank a guy. Would you like me to open the door for you and you can go out with the fucking zombies?" I start pressing numbers into the keypad, but her hand shoots over to mine, pushing it away. "That's what I thought. This way." I grab her hand and we make our way through the underground maze to the stairs that lead up to the stores.

Her gaze sweeps the empty shops, hallways and gaping spaces, "Where is everybody else?" her voice is a low whisper.

"I don't care about anybody else." My reply is a little harsher than I intended. "I just know that I have you here now, and you're safe."

I catch her wrist and pull her towards 'Summit and Stream'.

I'm banking on my knowledge of zombie movies as my 'how to survive a zombie apocalypse guide.'

The security gate is down, and I kick it, sending a shiver of screaming metal along the giant empty space.

"Don't!" she screams at me, her grip tightening and her large eyes darting across the suddenly intimidating empty space.

"It's locked." I pull on the giant padlock as if to prove the obvious—in her state, very little is sinking in.

"What are we going to do?"

"I know another way in." I grab her again, leading her towards the security doors and through the back corridors. Echoes and screams follow us as we hurry down the narrow laneways intersecting the underbelly of the mall.

We make it to the back door of the sports and camping shop just as a blood-curdling scream shrieks behind us.

"They're coming." Her voice is shrill, and I'm starting to worry that she may not make it through the night.

I push the door open to the back office. A small 'exit' sign hangs above the door burning a luminous neon green, making the darkened room feel eerie in the light.

Bangs and clanks follow us into the room, and she latches onto my arm, huddling closer.

"We're safe here," I force the reassurance through gritted teeth, trying to sooth her, but her grip only tightens. "They can't get inside."

Somewhere in the distance a metal door bangs, and she jumps into my arms. I close my arms around her, pulling her close. We stand silent for a minute, and the world stands still with us. I breathe her in, the fruity scent of her shampoo flooding my mind with something dangerously familiar before I can stop myself. My stupidity only has her pushing away from me.

"Sorry," I mumble, but I've already screwed up. She backs away from me and looks around us at the small office, jumping at every sound.

I try to placate her. "We're safe here."

"What the hell is going on?" she finally says, her voice broken and shrill.

"I don't know, but it looks like some kind of zombie apocalypse."

She gives me a long, pointed look. "Those don't happen in real life."

I shrug. "I can open the doors, and we can go look again." As if to punctuate my point another metal bang reverberates in the small space and she lets out a muted cry.

"Did Rob kill Laura?"

Hannah's gaze remains glued to the floor. Her chest jerks with every breath, her whole body trembling.

I reach for her hand, but she flinches away. "Hannah, look at me."

I try again, hands on her shoulders this time. She shoves them off. "Hannah, look at me."

She shakes her head, backing up a step. "Is Laura dead?"

"I don't know." The words taste wrong in my mouth. "I don't know." We can both hear the lie in my voice.

She grips her hair, fingers twisting.

"All I know is that I woke up to zombies in my house. I think my they killed my mum. All I could think about was finding you before it was too late, and I did. I *found* you. Only you."

"What about everyone else?"

"I don't know about everyone else. I don't *care* about anyone else."

"Ethan..."

"Hannah..." The silence between us is thick, too much unsaid. I don't push her on it. "We only have each other right now."

Her breath shudders. "My phone. Where is it? I need to call my parents. I need to call Laura."

She pats down her pockets, turning them inside out, getting more frantic by the second. But we both know where her phone is—on her nightstand, where she left it.

"Fuck, I don't have it." Her voice cracks. "Give me your phone. Quick."

I set it in her palm.

She dials.

Waits.

Tries again.

Her features twist, skin pulled tight, jaw trembling like it might unhinge.

"There's no signal." She stares at the screen, disbelief turning into something uglier. "It's *dead*." She throws it back at me like the useless piece of metal it is.

She paces. Her hands tug at her sleeves. "No, no, no, no."

The panic is rising fast, and I don't know how to stop it.

"This *can't* be happening," she says, voice climbing higher. "*What the fuck is going on?*"

"Hannah, I don't know, I'm not sure."

The words hang between us. Her eyes lose their frantic shine focusing on my face. Her lips tremble as her fear drains into something heavier, darker. Maybe she is starting to accept that I have no answers.

A breath.

A broken wailing sound.

"My parents. I need to call my parents."

She's searching herself again, but it's pointless. "*Shit.* I left it—"

"On your nightstand," I finish for her.

I unlock my phone again, hand it back to her.

She punches in a number.

Waits.

Nothing.

Tries again.

Nothing.

"There's no signal." Her fingers tighten around the phone before she hurls it onto the desk.

Silence.

She looks at me like I'm a stranger. Then, slowly, exhaustion starts to win.

"If they come inside..."

"I'll stay up," I promise. "In fact, I'll get us some supplies. Just in case."

"Supplies?"

"Weapons, shelter."

She follows me to the office door, her head jerking over her shoulder at every sound. "We should barricade the door."

It's heavy and metal and would likely survive a nuclear bomb but at least she is finally in survival mode.

I open the office door and we glue ourselves to the wall as we scan the dark shop. The glow of the exit signs illuminates everything in an eerie neon wash, casting long shadows that flicker with every breath.

"We need torches and batteries."

Her chin dips in a small, mechanical motion and she grabs my arm as I start moving towards the packed aisles. We move quickly past the active wear and a multitude of various balls, past the tennis rackets and shoes. I stop at the golf section and pick up a nine iron. She looks at me questioningly. "Weapon," I say as I swing it through the air. She moves when I do, no more words needed, then grabs one of her own, after a second she grabs two more.

We continue down the aisle till we get to the camping gear, I start grabbing items off shelves, throwing them in the middle of the aisle. Torches, batteries, sleeping bags, a tent. The pile grows quickly. Hannah won't release the clubs, standing like a soldier at the base of the pile keeping guard.

I start grabbing a handful of items. "Help me,"

She looks at me as if I've lost my mind thinking she'll

release the club, and I let out a low breath through my teeth, setting everything back down. I grab her wrist and yank her with me making a beeline for the entrance and grabbing a trolley. When we snake through the store once more, we pass the baseball section. I drop the club. It clatters noisily on the tiled floor making Hannah squeal.

"Sorry." I avoid her death stare and reach for a bat; it's wooden and heavy in my hands and reminds me of every single game I've never played, not at school, not as a child, not ever. Baseball was not a game for the likes of my family. I swing the bat telling myself I don't care what my dad's face would look like at the receiving end of the swing, then grab four others, throwing them into the trolley before heading back to our stash.

This time Hannah helps as we shove everything into the trolley and head back to the imagined safety of the office.

Digging into the bottom I grab the large lantern and insert the batteries, immediately the room bursts into light.

Hannah looks defeated and petrified clutching her club and leaning at the door of the office.

I set my bat gently on the table and unroll the four-person pop-up tent. The idea of pitching it indoors feels absurd, childish, even, but there's something quietly comforting about it. It's not just about sleep. It's about creating a boundary. A thin, zippered wall between us and the outside world.

Maybe it's ridiculous. But maybe that thin layer of baby blue plastic will give her the illusion of safety, of space, of choice, and that matters. I can't give her everything she needs, but for now, I can give her this. A small, enclosed sanctuary in the middle of a lie.

Even if it's flimsy, it still feels like shelter. And I'm still trying to be the guy who provides it.

The tent takes up most of the room in the cramped office. I pull the flaps aside and unroll the sleeping bags inside.

Once I am satisfied with my handy work I call Hannah over.

She doesn't move.

"Hannah." She's frozen in place, shock and fear concreting her feet to the floor.

I walk over to her. As I take her hand, she flinches, and I think she may swing the club at me. "Hannah, you're safe."

Her face tells me that she doesn't believe me in the slightest, and yet her shoulders slump a fraction as I lead her to the tent.

She collapses onto the floor, sitting down and staring at nothing. She looks mildly more relieved, and a flicker of relief stirs in me at having pacified her, even if it's short-lived and meaningless. The guilt has already started to gnaw at me.

The room is deathly quiet, now that all the unusual sounds have vanished.

"Get some sleep, I'll keep watch."

She hesitates, then folds in on herself, curling up in the sleeping bag, arms wrapped tight around the golf club.

She doesn't look at me again.

It takes almost an hour before her breathing evens out and she falls asleep, and I am alone at the end of the world with the most beautiful girl I've ever known.

Finally I might get to fix the worst mistake of my life.

6. The way things were

Ethan

Leaning against the wall I watch Hannah, mesmerised by the subtle rhythm of her breathing as she mumbles in her sleep.

Hannah Jones has always been the most beautiful girl in the world. I thought this from the moment I laid eyes on her twenty-five years ago, and I still believe it today. Every detail about that moment burns clear in my memory, her crooked little smile, nine little freckles that danced across her nose and the wild hair that seemed like it hadn't been brushed in months. There she was, swinging back and forth, her untamed mane blowing behind her, giggling her head off without a worry in the world.

I wasn't supposed to be there that day. I wasn't supposed to be anywhere with *these* types of people, as Mother called them.

It was my tenth birthday, and just like every single one before it, Mother had invited all her rich snooty friends who paid me no heed and couldn't care less about the fact that I was alive. All they cared about was that Edward and Eveline Vale invited them to *their* party, that they were in their good books and good graces. Of course, they showed up and gave me a token present I could do nothing with, then chased my father around for the rest of the day talking business and money.

Grandad was just like him, mostly, until recently. Something had changed in him, thawed. He watched me standing in the corner in the ridiculous navy blue suit a ten-year-old should not be wearing, wavering on the verge of tears and trying to keep it together. The Vales didn't cry at parties, or ever. Emotion was weakness and not allowed. I was to be grateful for what I had.

He crossed the room and took my hand.

No one noticed as we slipped outside and walked away from the property.

No one cared that we crossed the threshold of my parent's ridiculous estate and towards the town.

No one entertained the thought of the two of us stumbling upon this playground, but there we were, and as I stood near the edge of the fence watching other kids play, my stomach fluttered and my feet itched to run to them, to be just like them.

I looked at his face then, the question written in my eyes, his smile was so warm, so strange, so unlike him, but it gave me all the permission I needed as he released my hand and walked over to a bench.

I took a deep breath and started walking toward the swing, my legs feeling like jelly. I knew I didn't blend in, not when all their clothes were £10 t-shirts and shorts while I was wearing £300 shoes. I felt like the outsider they thought I was, the weight of their stares heavy on my tiny shoulders.

Most of the adults had stopped talking, their eyes pinned me in place.

I glanced over my shoulder at Grandad, who jutted his chin forward, urging me to continue. Vales don't back down, they don't cower. My insides tangled with nerves as I neared the swing.

"Do you want to play? Come on, push me on the swing." Her voice cut through my nerves.

She was standing in front of me. Shorter than I was, but those beautiful big brown eyes were looking directly into my soul and that smile—I've never stopped loving it.

The girl took my hand and led me towards the swings, sat down and grinned the entire time as I started pushing. She giggled, and I thought right there and then my ten-year-old heart would stop beating because it was the most beautiful sound I'd ever heard. Maybe it's dramatic, but I remember it as something bigger than it was, a moment polished and preserved in my museum of memories. Even after all this time, this is how I see her; the girl who used to be my best friend. The girl who used to be my everything, till I fucked it all up.

By all rights, I shouldn't have been there. I should have stayed in my palace above the town filled to the brim with overpriced food and stuck-up people made mostly of plastic, but I was there with her, against all odds. We should never have been friends, not according to the adults.

Her family wasn't like ours; we were too different. My family basically owned this town; my great, great grandfather built it and named it after our family. Valenwood. Sometimes I cringe thinking about it, wishing my name could be associated with something else other than branding an entire town, an entire community.

But back then as a kid, I didn't understand any of these

things, I wasn't meant to. We all start out equally, there's no colour, no religion, no poverty line, none of it matters as a kid, all you see is a friend, another human. But as we grow and mature and go to school and form our own thoughts, twisted and influenced by social media, teachers, and our parents, we draw these lines inside ourselves. Lines around other people, lines that should be invisible and not matter but somehow, they do.

The day I met her, there were no lines. There were no clouds in the sky and it was a beautiful blue as I pushed her on the swing and she laughed and laughed and laughed. Her hair fell back, tickling the back of her neck, her dress flew up-and-down, and her stupid big boots covered in mud swung back-and-forth. That might have been one of the happiest moments of my life.

"My name is Hannah, Hannah Jones, what's your name?"

"My name is Ethan." I was about to give her my last name but something inside me stopped. I stumbled and bit my tongue. Maybe some part of me knew that there were lines to be crossed even if I didn't understand exactly why.

Maybe it was the fact that her clothes looked a little bit more faded and worn like they'd managed to survive dozens of washes, and yet, there was a little stain on the hip that almost blended in like a flower but wasn't. Maybe it was the fact that I was in a suit with my shirt bleached too white, my hair combed perfectly to one side, or that I didn't have dirt under my nails like she did. Whatever it was, I just knew that I didn't belong.

I gave her a goofy smile as she grabbed my hand and led us to the slide. "Come on!"

Despite the sting, I catch myself smiling at the memory.

7. Everything is sinking in

02/11/2025
Ethan

I wake up to rattling and reach for the bat that lays limply on the floor by my side. I'm not sure when exactly I fell asleep.

"Sorry, I didn't mean to wake you." Her tone suggests otherwise.

"It's fine. Sorry I fell asleep."

"Lucky you," she mumbles quiet but barbed as if *she* got no sleep, barely acknowledging my apology.

Hannah crawls out of her sleeping bag, grabs it and wraps herself in it, keeping warm. Makes sense. When I tore her out of her house last night, she was in an old T-shirt and a pair of tiny shorts. Not exactly apocalypse attire, but damn if her long legs don't look great in them.

She makes her way to me and comes to a stand at the door of the security office. Her gaze flickers over the large desolate space. In the morning light the shop looks strangely comforting, full aisles of sports goods. Except that the shop

🖋 61 🖋

stands barren where it should be overrun by families and aspiring athletes.

I push myself up and stretch my stiff legs. I didn't intend on falling asleep like a pretzel in the doorway, and my large frame clearly doesn't appreciate it.

There are noises coming from outside, bangs and growls.

Turns out apocalypses don't take breaks.

"We need to barricade the doors." Determination laces her voice.

For a second I want to argue—the doors are all bolted shut with state-of-the-art locks, metal upon metal and a foolproof design that would keep a tank out, but Hannah doesn't need to know that. Keeping her occupied is keeping her mind safe—not asking too many questions.

"Barricades are a great idea. Lead the way."

She looks at me like I've attempted to push her down a canyon, and she clutches her nine iron before turning away. I stupidly understand my mistake and catch up in a few strides, taking the lead.

The metal roller door of the sports shop screams as it rolls up and opens a gaping hole to our sanctuary, the cool mall air shoves itself in our faces, and there is a second where our sudden exposure snaps a shiver down my spine at our vulnerability. Hannah instinctively tucks herself behind me, and a sensation of wicked pleasure trickles inside me. A part of her still sees me as her protector, her saviour—her anything—and that's a good start.

Our first port of call are the giant glass doors that show us the world beyond the boundary of safety I've created for us.

Our steps echo strangely in the giant empty cavity. Usually, this place would be full of laughter and voices, background music, and even the undertone white noise of the air con and vending machines, but everything is frozen in time, silent and deadly. Chills crawl along my skin as we steal our way towards the entrance.

My jaw hangs slack as I look at the aftermath of last night.

The late morning sun hangs lazily in a perfectly clear blue sky making the scene outside even more surreal. Everything is eerily still, too quiet. The parking lot lies, deserted with cars scattered at odd angles, some left with doors ajar as if their owners bolted mid-parking. Shopping carts tipped on their sides, abandoned like afterthoughts. Empty food wrappers, loose receipts, and scattered grocery bags drift across the asphalt, rustling in the faint wind.

Around the edges of the lot, bushes and small trees sway slightly, casting long, creeping shadows on the ground. Not a single car drives by. No signs of life. Despite the oddness of it all, there's a certain sense of calm. I can almost breathe but just as I draw in a long inhale—a loud *thud* makes me jump out of my skin.

Next to me, Hannah leaps backwards with a squeal as a figure hits the window in front of us with sudden, bone-chilling force. It's Rob. Or... what used to be him. His face is pressed against the glass, hard enough to distort his features, eyes vacant and unfocused. His arms smack the door, fingers scratching and scraping, smudging the clear surface. There's no snarl, no rage—just a hollow persistence as if he's unaware of the barrier between us and him. The impact rattles the pane, sending an unexpected jolt of tension through the mall's hollow silence.

I turn to Hannah, who's buried herself in the safety of the sleeping bag, with only her face poking through like a turtle. I'd be laughing if she didn't look petrified. We lock eyes for just a second, a silent understanding between us. "Let's go."

I find Hannah's hand behind the thick material and steer her away to the nearest trolley bay where we push the heavy stack together towards the front door. We line the heavy trolleys in front of the door and return moments later with locks and chains found in the camp store.

We work tirelessly throwing anything vaguely barricade-worthy in front of doors and exits—chairs, tables, and even a few potted plants, like we're in some amateur production of *Zombie Siege*. And I guess in many ways we are.

At some point, she shrugs off the sleeping bag before tossing it aside. Her skin's flushed now, cheeks pink from exertion and the afternoon sun pouring through the large shop windows. The t-shirt and shorts that once screamed unprepared now look almost fitting, like she's adapted, like this is who she is now.

I jam the last pot plant in sight against the fire door and run my hands on my jeans. They're sore and sweaty from the amount of moving and lifting we've done, and my shirt clings to my skin as a patch of sweat develops along my back.

"Check it again." Hannah looks at my back pocket. A part of me wishes the look is her checking out my very fine ass, but alas, I know what she really wants is the phone that I've stuffed in there.

I pull it out and try to search for a signal holding it out in every direction. "Nothing."

She leaps forward and grabs the phone from me in a quick, desperate motion. Maybe she's convinced her magical touch might somehow revive the reception.

"Urgh, this thing is useless." She throws it at me and it nearly slips out of my sweaty palms.

"Then why do you keep asking for it?"

She stares at me for a second, then shakes her head. "Because someone might be trying to reach us. Because there might be *something* out there. A message. An alert. A map. I don't know!"

She opens the space between us, taking a step away and turns back. "What even happened, Ethan? Was it chemical? Biological? None of this makes any sense."

I stay silent, and she gestures toward the phone again.

"Why are we the only ones left? Why didn't we turn? What makes us different? And how are you so fucking calm?" She presses her fingers to her temples, voice thinning out. "What if it's not over? What if it hasn't even started yet?"

"Losing it won't get us anywhere."

She looks at me like I've slapped her. "So that's what you think I'm doing? Losing it?"

I lift my hands up, palms out, like I'm trying to steady the air between us. "That's not what I'm saying. I'm just as lost as you are."

"At least I'm trying to figure out what's going on."

"By building barricades?" The frustration finally leaks from my voice.

She glares at me before storming off towards the camping shop. I shove the phone back in my pocket and make to follow, then think better of it.

Maybe she'll finally accept that there's no Wi-Fi, no cell service. Just her and me in this oversized fortress of consumerism, the rest of the world supposedly in shambles, and the only connection between us is, well, us.

I leave her alone. The end of the world isn't easy to

process. She's lost everything she knows, everyone she loves. I give her the space I think she needs.

The barricades are solid enough to buy us some time if anyone actually tries to get in. I stretch out my back and wipe the sweat from my forehead. Every door and fire exit are now jammed with chairs, tables, shopping trolleys, and potted plants.

I head toward the security tunnel and make my way toward one of the supermarkets. I let myself in and make my way through the eerily still aisles, fluorescent lights hanging dead above me. The place still carries the lingering scent of baked bread, ripe produce, and sharp cleaning chemicals—faintly mixed with the cool, stale hush of air that hasn't moved in hours.

I head straight for the basics. A couple of towels, soap, toothbrushes. I grab a few other things—deodorant, a hair-brush, a packet of wet wipes. There's something quietly reassuring about it, like if we can just rinse the sweat off our faces and scrape the day from our teeth, maybe we can trick ourselves into feeling normal. More human. Like the world hasn't gone completely off the rails.

On my way out, I spot a rack of sleepwear. Cotton tees, flannel pants, some tank tops folded neatly in stacks. I grab a few, guessing Hannah's size. There's a fleece hoodie too—pink, obnoxious, but warm, and I tuck that under my arm.

I find the nearest bathrooms, those cold, echoey ones near the food court, and flick the tap until it sputters to life. I remove my shirt and bend low over the sink and let the cold water run over the back of my neck, then tilt my head allowing it to pour across my scalp and down my face. It's a jolt at first, sharp enough to steal my breath, but I don't pull away. I let it run, let it sting. It feels like penance.

For a second, I stand still.

Head bowed.

Eyes shut.

Breathe in.

A shiver snakes down my spine, sharp and illicit.

Breathe out.

My chest tightens with what I shouldn't feel.

Breathe in.

Something dark hums under my skin.

Breathe out.

The water trickling past my ears the only sound in the room, which somehow makes everything else feel quieter too.

Then I reach for my newly acquired face wash and scrub at my face, chasing off the grime and all the parts of myself I'd rather not sit with right now. It doesn't fix anything—but it helps me pretend, for a minute, that I'm still the kind of guy who knows what the hell he's doing.

When I look up, water dripping from my chin, I catch my reflection in the mirror. With no overhead lights, only a faint wash of daylight slants in from the hall, bending my features just enough to make me look like a stranger, paler than usual, eyes a little too dark. Like someone trying to hold it together while something cracks beneath the surface.

"What the hell are you doing?" I mutter. The guy staring back has no idea.

I dry off with the towel, shove everything into the bag, and head straight to the camping store. I grab an inflatable mattress, an extra sleeping bag, some extra pillows and a lantern, one of those battery-powered ones that looks as if it could last a few days if the power situation doesn't improve.

I find Hannah in the office, sitting in the tent, chin on her knees, cheeks streaked with dried tears. I pretend not to notice as I toss the camping supplies on the floor. "I bring comfort."

She wipes her face, gets up and moves out of my way, leaning against the door frame, her hands folded, watching me as I inflate the mattress and wrestle to get it into the tent. She hasn't smiled once since yesterday.

"Guess we're roughing it in style," I say, patting my handy work. "If the world's ending, at least we've got... glamping?"

She doesn't reply. Instead, she picks up the lantern, inspecting it with a frown as if it's somehow not apocalypse-proof enough.

"Electricity's still out." I state the obvious, watching her face. "Food and water supply are fine for now, but if this keeps up... I don't know how long the meat will last." I gesture toward the hallway where the food court lies dormant.

She doesn't respond to that either, which I half-expected. She brushes past me and sits on the mattress.

I reach for the other bag and hand it to her. "For you. Towels. Soap. Clothes..."

She eyes the bag, then me. Doesn't move.

"This isn't ours," she says flatly.

"Neither is all the stuff we grabbed last night."

"That was different."

I raise an eyebrow in a silent question.

"It was an emergency."

"And what's this?" I cast my hands across the empty store and the void left by the lack of people in the mall.

She shrugs, obviously lost.

I release a slow breath, dragging a hand through my hair. "It's not *anyone's* anymore. Look around, Hannah. No staff, no customers. No power. The place is a graveyard."

She pulls her knees in closer, not looking at me. "We don't know that. We don't know who made it out. This belongs to someone."

I almost say it. Almost tell her that we both know I can buy the whole damn store twice over without blinking. That none of this even scratches the surface. But I swallow my words. She's never cared about that. And I've never wanted her to.

"Look, I'm not looting flat screens or designer shoes. I'm trying to make this slightly less unbearable."

She doesn't say anything, but her face is marred in guilt. Like using a toothbrush is going to doom her soul. She pulls the bag closer anyway but doesn't open it.

I stand there for a second longer, then sigh. "Suit yourself. I'm gonna go find us some breakfast."

Turning, I and walk out before I let the irritation surface on my face.

I'm tired.

I'm trying. And somehow it still feels like the ground between us is cracking.

I know I've got my work cut out for me, there's no quick fix for a broken heart, no bandage for betrayal. But for now, there's just the two of us, trapped in this hollowed-out world, and every moment that stretches between us is another chance to make things right—even if she's not ready to see it yet.

8. Not giving up... being sensible

2/11/2025
Ethan

Hannah finds me in the neon lit food hall normally bustling with impatient shoppers and greasy burger wrappers, but today it's eerily quiet. She flinches at every sound and her head jerks backwards with every other step. She's wearing the pink hoodie and a pair of flannel pants.

"Nice hoodie."

She sneers at me. "Some would say hideous."

"Some would." I look around dramatically. "Lucky there's no one around to worry about your poor fashion choices."

Her eyes narrow, I change tact.

"Hungry?"

"Starving."

"What would you like?" I wave my hand around the food hall where every possible combination of food has its place. "Take your pick"

She shrugs, her glazed eyes scanning the possibilities.

"How about a burger?" My gaze lands on the burger stall across from us.

She leans in. "When have you ever cooked a burger?" I bite back my smile, getting a hint of minty freshness from her breath.

"Hey, I cook for myself I'll have you know."

"Really? What about your 'people'." She does a brilliant impression of my mother, and I crack up.

"Only Mother has 'people'. *I* have skills"

"Debatable."

"And provable."

I wink at her as I get up and make my way behind the counter. The grill and fries both work on gas and are easily lit. I let them warm up while I make my way to the back end of the shop and grab a couple of burgers, buns, and frozen chips. I get to work, and the space begins to fill with the smell of cooked meat and greasy chips. My own stomach churns, empty after almost 24 hours without food.

"What a pro." Hannah leans over the counter, her hair falling over her face. My heart rate spikes, hands tightening around the spatula.

"Told you." I smile at her and scan the barren food hall. "Think you could find us a table?"

She cracks the faintest of smiles, and a warmth spreads through my chest. Finally a chink in the ice, even if it's just a barely-there fracture.

She pushes away from the counter and makes as if she is looking around, then settles for the table nearest the stall. Safety in numbers, I guess.

I bring the food over, setting the plate in front of her. Hannah eyes it sceptically.

"Only the best for our... post-apocalyptic paradise." I sit across from her. "Surviving with style, right?"

She snorts, barely looking up from her meal. "Yeah, a real paradise. Nothing like artificial meat and plastic trays to make a girl swoon."

I grin, savouring the sarcasm in her voice. "Hey, I'm doing my best here. It's not every day you get to... you know, sweep someone off their feet while the world ends around you."

She looks up, a flash of something in her eyes, but just as quickly, she drops her gaze back to her plate. It's a look that holds a thousand things she's not ready to say, things I'm probably not ready to hear either. We eat the rest of our meal in silence, each of us eyeing the other in the dim, fading light.

When I'm done, I push away the tray and lean back in my chair. "So... not bad, right?" I say, hoping for a small win.

She raises an eyebrow, taking her last bite. "Let's just say if the zombies don't get us, your cooking might."

"Ouch."

She sucks away the grease on her fingers, and I shift in my seat, fully aware that it's just Hannah and I in this large space. For a second she was my Hannah again, snarky and sweet all at once.

"So, what's the plan?" She pushes away from the table and studies my face.

"You mean dessert?"

Her eyes narrow, razor-edged and dangerous, all the humour drained from her features. "What are we going to do?"

I sigh, leaning against the table. "Right now? We stay put. We've got supplies, a safe spot... It makes sense to hunker down until things settle."

Her laugh is short and humourless. She glances away.

"Hunker down? That's your brilliant plan? Just sit here while—who knows what—is going on out there?"

I hold my hands up. "Look, rushing into chaos isn't going to do either of us any good. We're safe here. We have food, water, shelter. It's better than risking it out there without knowing what we're facing."

"What about the electricity?"

"Still out."

"But the lights around us are still on." She waves her hand towards the emergency exit signs.

"It's just the emergency lights; they run off a generator."

"So we can redirect the power, turn on the TV and see what's out there."

"The generators are in the basement. We don't know what's down there. Also I don't have a mechanical engineering degree and I don't want to electrocute myself, or worse, switch off the little power we have."

"So, we just sit here and what? Rot? Wait it out?"

I don't answer right away, and she presses harder.

"Do you even know what this is?" she asks, voice rising. "Is it a virus? Is it airborne? Is it in the water? Why did everyone turn except us? My parents—Laura—everyone just... gone? And we're supposed to just sit here with that?"

"How would I know? Hannah. It's not like I've done this before, but we can give it a few days at least. We have no idea what's going on. For now, we're safe. We're together."

She looks at me like I've just said something pathetic.

"So what, you don't want to try and find out? Don't you want answers? Don't you want to know *why* we're not like them?"

I open my mouth, but she keeps going.

"What if we're sick and just haven't turned yet? What if

someone out there knows what happened? What if some-one's looking for us?"

"If we were sick, we'd already know."

"So, you're just giving up?" She takes her tray and throws it across the room. It clatters against the tiles, echoing in the huge cavern.

"It's not giving up, it's being sensible…"

She shakes her head, clearly unconvinced. "We can't just sit around like this. We need a plan, we need to get out of here!"

Tears stream down her cheeks coloured with anger and frustration. "We need to go." Her voice breaks, and I can't hold myself back any longer. I rush over to her, cradling her in my arms, pulling her close. She doesn't resist, wrapping herself around me as her smaller body quakes against mine, her tears soaking my shirt.

"It'll be okay."

"It won't. I'm scared. I'm struggling to stay calm." Her voice breaks against my aching chest as guilt and sadness floods my senses.

"*We'll* be okay. I have you." I pull her closer still. "We've always said we'll be here for one another at the end of the world…"

At that, she pushes herself away from me, her reddened wet eyes latch on to mine briefly. "Those weren't the words we used." She grinds the words through clenched teeth and turns to walk away.

"Hannah."

She flinches at the sudden noise and recovers quickly, walking away, and leaving me staring after her, a knot of frustration tightening in my chest.

9. Day 2

03/11/25
Ethan

Hannah finds me in the food hall. Like me, she makes a beeline for the smoothie bar. There is still plenty of ripe fruit, muesli and yogurt which hasn't gone off just yet. She fills up a bowl and comes to sit at my table.

She slouches into the chair, shoulders loose, a quiet stillness settling over her, no hint of yesterday's tension, as if all her fears evaporated in her sleep.

"How did you sleep?"

"I would say like the dead but..." She waves her hand toward the other end of the mall where the doors are sealed and barricaded. A part of me is relieved at her attempt at humour. "So," she falls into her seat, "why did you do it?"

My eyes dart to her face, my chest tightens and my hand trembles dropping my spoon into my sloppy breakfast. "Do what?"

"Why did you really come back to town?"

I shift in my seat. "You know why I'm back." My tone is cooler than I intended.

"Okay, I'll rephrase, I know why you came." Her voice steadies, lower now, her gaze fixed on mine.. "Why did you stay? I know it's not to spend quality time with your mother."

"No."

"So why are you here?"

I clear my throat. "To save the company, be all the things my dad wanted me to be."

"Bullshit. I'm not the press or some tabloid you have to impress. Are you running away from something?"

"No, nothing to run from my parents can't cover up."

"So why?"

"I just needed a fresh start, in a familiar place."

She folds her arms, eyes narrowing. "How about the truth?"

I sigh, leaning back into my chair. "My family has always taken. They've raped and pillaged this town at every turn, they've depleted everything good and mostly just bought misery to everyone." She's nodding in agreement, not even trying to defend them. And somehow, that stings. It's the truth, but it's still my family, and my ego doesn't take the hit lightly.

"Anyway, with Dad passing and the company in need of a new head, I thought I could take the reins and maybe just shift direction. Maybe do something good for a change, something meaningful, like you." Her eyes grow a little wider as I speak, and I track her expression wondering which part of my answer surprised her most.

"Teaching is overrated." She shrugs as if to rid herself from my compliment.

"It's one of the most important jobs in the world."

"Sure, maybe. Maybe if I was teaching younger kids full of potential, setting their foundations and making a real difference in their lives instead of teaching a bunch of spoiled, smelly, pervy teenagers."

"Oh, don't blame the teenagers. I bet if you were my teacher I'd perve over you too." I wink at her and watch her shoulders bunch up and her face twist in part disgust, part amusement.

"Ew, that's gross. I don't want to think about my students like that."

"I bet they think about you like that all the time, 'oh miss Jones...'" She throws her spoon at me, and I just manage to dodge it before she gets up, taking a few back-wards steps.

No matter how much I try to bridge the gap between us, she keeps her distance.

"That's not funny."

"Come on, Hannah, it's a little funny. There's nothing wrong with an innocent crush."

She mumbles something under her breath.

"What's that?"

"You wouldn't know the first thing about innocence." She raises her voice at me.

"Of course I do."

She pulls a face, rolling her eyes. "Sure, *Barethrone*."

I'm taken aback by her response, but unlikely for any of the reasons she's thinking. "You heard about that?"

"Everyone did! That and about your other adventures; Peep Show Prince, Valenwood Flasher, Exposeur..."

A smile plays on my face as she lists my indiscretions.

"What are you laughing about?"

"I'm just flattered that you kept tabs on me all these years." I lean casually back into my chair.

"I didn't keep tabs." Her arms tighten across her chest.

"Stalked then."

"I haven't been stalking you!"

"Sure, whatever you say." A spark of satisfaction prickles along my spine as the colour rises up her neck and spread across her face. I don't care if it's embarrassment or anger, it's fucking beautiful.

"Whatever. I couldn't help it even if I wanted to. Every time you fucked some girl in an alley it was all over the news." Her face turns a shade of red and her nostrils flare.

My smile spreads. My girl is jealous *and* busted. "No they weren't. I'll give you Peepshow Prince—that one was a disaster, but my parents paid good money to those newspapers to make any other pictures and stories vanish. In fact, only a few vague, bizarre, off the cut, small, unheard of magazines or tabloids may have published one or two. Someone would have to go out of their way to find them..." I lean forward in my seat and hold her stare. "Stalker."

The red on her cheeks deepens and her beautiful eyes widen for a moment before she huffs away. "I don't have time for this. We have *actual* issues to deal with!" she snaps, her voice tinged with frustration. "And I need a new spoon."

I can't help but smile. As I watch her storm off, a giddy amusement bubbles inside me—this unexpected revelation has made my morning much more entertaining.

I enjoy the rest of my breakfast even if I eat it without her company. The idea that Hannah has been keeping tabs on me makes me skittish and gives me a sense of hope that maybe there could still be something between us and that spark we shared hasn't entirely gone out.

I find her back in our makeshift bunker, her head hanging over the mattress, staring at the ceiling. I take in her large brown eyes and shapely body, the auburn hair frazzled around her in a messy crazed way. She sighs heavily at my approach.

Walking into the office, I ignore her tightening jaw and turn my attention to rummaging through the desk drawers. At the bottom of the disorganised drawer, I find a rubber stress ball.

"Perfect." I raise my prize triumphantly and make my way back to the door frame where I slide down and take my allocated place.

I squeeze the ball.

It lets out a faint squeak.

Hannah looks up, glaring. I swallow my smile and squeeze again.

Squeeze. Release. Squeak.

Squeeze. Release. Squeak.

She sighs. Loudly. I don't respond. Just pretend to be busy while watching her out of the corner of my eye.

She huffs again, more pointed this time as if the very air offends her.

I don't bite. I keep working the ball, while she keeps pretending I don't exist.

She shifts noisily on the mattress, then stands up and walks over to the desk. She starts fiddling with the computer monitor, unplugging, replugging, tapping at the dead keyboard like maybe, something will flicker to life and distract her from the unbearable fact of my presence.

"Still dead," I say, not looking up.

She ignores me.

Opens a drawer.

Closes it.

Picks up a stapler.

Puts it back down.

Another theatrical huff. She's probably pissed that I found the squeaking stress ball before she did.

I fight back a smile while releasing the ball deliberately slowly, stretching out its annoying squeak.

She rolls her eyes and crosses the room to check the emergency exit light, like it might let her out into a world not full of zombies. When that shockingly doesn't happen, she drops onto the mattress with an exaggerated flop, groaning into her hands like the universe has personally wronged her.

A full thirty seconds pass before she mutters, "I'm bored."

I glance up. "You sure? I thought the monitor revival ritual was keeping you busy."

She bares her teeth at me, and I can't hold back, my mouth splitting in an amused smile.

"Want to go outside?" I ask, stretching like I'm actually considering it. "I hear there's plenty to do; screaming, panicking, maybe some light running for your life."

She levels me with a death glare.

"No?" I feign innocence.

She rolls her eyes, annoyed but not enough to leave the room.

"Well," I shrug, "we've got a whole mall to ourselves. We can go exploring."

She raises a brow. "Exploring?"

"Yeah," A grin tugs at the corner of my mouth, "I'll protect you."

"I don't need you to protect me."

Somewhere outside something clangs, and she flinches. I want to comfort her, but she sheds off the fear and slides by me, her shoulder checking my chest as she does, pretending she's unperturbed.

"Let's go."

I follow her to the main hall.

10. Slipping into a new reality

Ethan

The mall feels surreal. Every shop open to us and not a soul around to care.

I glance over at Hannah as she wanders down the main hall, taking in the empty stores and the bizarre quiet that fills the space. She pads across the floor, slow and thoughtful, as she peers into one display after another. Endless clothing shops with name brand items. It's never really been her thing. She brushes past the make-up counters and jewellery stalls as if she can't see them.

I've always appreciated that about her. Hannah isn't image driven and, money—though a necessity for everyone —has never been her main concern. She knows exactly who she is and is comfortable in her own skin, even when she wears affordable unbranded clothes. She likes comfort and substance over fancy shit. It's part of how I knew, back then, she was with me for who I was and not who my family is or the size of my inheritance.

I catch up to her. "Alright, what's it gonna be? Full mall, no rules."

She shrugs, shooting me an unreadable look. "Maybe some earplugs? Those would be useful right now."

I laugh. "Ouch. But I meant something fun, not anti-Ethan gear."

Her pace doesn't slow, but her tone shifts. Sharper. "The end of the world isn't supposed to be *fun*."

I match her stride. "Says who?" I gesture broadly at the empty mall around us. "It's the apocalypse, we get to make our own rules."

She looks at me sideways, one brow raised. "And your first move is to be as loud and obnoxious as possible?"

I grin. "I'm just trying to improve morale."

She rolls her eyes. "And I'm trying to survive this apocalypse." Her lips quirk up at the corners and she keeps walking, steering us into a furniture store.

We glance around the spotless displays like we're actually considering buying a new couch. My heart twinges at the thought, there was a time I believed that would be a possibility; Hannah and me till the end of the world in our own home. I push away the thoughts and scan the enormous space.

Hannah's eyes catch on a massive bed, pristine with thick, fluffy duvets, and I follow her stare, a slow grin spreading across my lips as I toe off my shoes.

"What are you doing?"

I don't answer but make a beeline for the bed. I jump on it with force, sending the beautifully set pillows flying across the floor. I get to my feet and start bounding, the mattress sinking and springing under my weight.

She raises an eyebrow. "Seriously? Aren't you a little old for that?"

"You might be," I shoot back and see that spark of annoyance flashing across her face. Hannah doesn't like to lose and, even though this isn't a competition, I know I've set a challenge she won't pass by.

"I'm younger than you!"

"By four months," I breathe out. "What's wrong, Hannah? Afraid I'll jump higher?"

"You're not going to bait me with that pathetic threat."

"Okay, grumpy grandma, suit yourself."

At that she shoots me a long look. It's not angry but, in that moment, she knows she will either have to come jump on this bed or be forever known as grumpy grandma.

She rolls her eyes, then kicks off her slides before hopping up beside me, muttering, "I'm doing this under protest."

"Sure you are." I smirk, and we start jumping.

Each leap we attempt to out jump the other, sending us springing up and down with all the reckless abandon only a child could muster. Instantly, I am flooded with a thousand memories, and they threaten to drown me as I watch her hair bounce around her smiling face.

I don't know when we start to laugh, but suddenly we're both giddy and laughter spills out as the mattress creaks under us.

Hannah's face transforms. The worry lines that have set in over the last two days turn to laughter lines. It's the first time since I've been back in town that Hannah is laughing. Its genuine and sweet and possibly the most beautiful sound in the world right now, and my heart rockets in my chest. I can't decide if it's the jumping or Hannah that's making me breathless.

Bouncing up I land awkwardly, losing my balance. I tumble onto the bed, the uneven weight making Hannah trip also and she falls in a heap above me. We collapse in a tangle of laughter, lungs burning, rolling on our backs to breathe again.

"Wow, I didn't know grandmas could still have so much fun."

"Wow, congratulations on outperforming a grandma. Be proud," she throws at me through haggard breaths.

Leaning on my elbow, I prop my head up, still catching my breath. "I'm all about performance, baby."

"Yeah, I bet you put on a *super* show."

"Want front row tickets?" I wiggle my eyebrows at her.

She shifts onto her side with a dry snort. "I'd rather watch the zombies eat Edna Crabbs."

"The old crone that used to live across from the playground?"

"One and the same."

"I mean, yeah, the woman was mean as hell but... Wow, cold."

"She threw tomatoes at us while we were swinging."

I gasp dramatically. "She was giving healthy snacks to young hungry kids."

Hannah rolls over, eyebrows arched sharply, lips pressed into a thin line, and her eyes narrow just enough to make it clear she's questioning whether I've lost my mind.

"Fine, let her be eaten, she probably would have outjumped you anyway."

She drags a pillow under her head. "Pppff. She moved away a few years back, got dementia. Her kids put her somewhere she can be cared for."

Hannah stops talking abruptly as if realising how normal our conversation is, how easily she has fallen into telling me the things that matter, how nostalgic all of this feels, pulling us back to before.

I don't want her to withdraw again, to close back up. "You know," I roll around a bit, "This bed is far more comfortable than that blow-up mattress in the camp shop."

"Then maybe you should sleep here instead."

"Then who will protect you?"

"From you?"

I glance over, exaggerating a wounded look. Her face is flushed, and her smile is beautiful.

"You don't need to be afraid of me, Hannah." Before I can stop myself, my hand—of its own volition—travels over to her face and removes a stray hair.

I tuck it behind her ear, and for a split-second the world stands still.

The touch of her skin under my fingers, the way her eyes grow, glued to mine.

For that instant it's just Hannah and me, like it's always been.

But just as I try to capture the moment and hold onto it, she rolls over and slips out the bed leaving me to fall onto my back and stare at the ceiling, finding my breath and settling my stammering heart.

Hannah straightens and grabs her slides. Taking her cue I trail her out to the main hall as she drifts toward the next shop: a bookstore.

Inside, the air is heavy with the smell of paper and leather, as though the place has held its breath waiting for someone to break the silence. Hannah wanders off into one of the aisles, trailing her fingers along the spines of books. She plucks a few out, flips through pages thoughtfully, and then glances over her shoulder at me.

"Here." She tosses me a thick novel. '*The End of the World: Tactics and Techniques, for Surviving any apocalypse.*'

I look over the book; it's heavy and bulky. "What am I meant to do with this? Beat the zombies over the head with it?"

She just shrugs, a faint smile on her lips. "Or read it to them, they might die of boredom listening to your voice."

"Wow. Are you saying I am a weapon of mass *distraction*?" I wiggle my eyebrows at her, impressed with my own quick wit.

She glances away with a shake of her head, but I don't miss the smile curling at her lips "Oh, I don't know about *mass*... maybe minor distraction at best." She winks at me, and my insides melt.

"Nothing minor about this weapon." I wave at myself as she attempts to cover her laugh with a cough.

"Mmmmm..." She looks me up and down as if assessing my potential. "A little less 'weapon,' a lot more 'novelty item'."

"Hey, I can inflict damage."

"Only if you count collateral damage." She's joking, but her words hold a scathing edge.

I huff in response not wanting to ruin this moment we're having by saying the wrong thing as Hannah lingers at shelves, reading the back of books, admiring covers and flipping through pages. She finally picks herself a couple; a murder mystery and a romance novel.

"Those are too thin to be weaponised."

"It's my brain that's the weapon in this scenario."

"Oh yeah?" I snatch the romance novel from her hand looking at the towering, brooding, broad-shouldered man on the cover. "What part of your brain does this stimulate?"

"The part that cares about... *hugging*"

"Are you planning on *hugging* the zombies to death?"

She snatches it back, a shade of red tinting her cheeks. "Even zombies deserve to be loved."

With that she walks out of the shop having had the final word.

Again.

We stumble into a clothing store. It's one of those outrageously expensive specialty stores that cater for special occasions, housing over-the-top dresses and colourful suits that look like they were designed by a five-year-old on a sugar rush.

Hannah eyes a rack of dresses. Her face twists and her eyes narrow as if she is trying to work out what it is she is actually looking at; half sceptical, half intrigued. A smile tugs at my mouth, and I can't help but watch her.

"It must be time," I say voice solemn.

Hannah turns to look at me, a raised eyebrow asking a silent question.

"To get our apocalypse outfits. I mean, is it even an apocalypse if you don't have an outfit?"

"Seriously?"

Grinning, I attempt to throw on a bright cherry-red jacket, which is clearly two sizes too small. I grunt as I force my arms into the too-tight, too-short sleeves. "Survival's one thing, but surviving in style?"

Hannah stifles a laugh. "Sure, if you call that style," she eyes my choice with a crooked curl of her lips.

"What would you call it?"

"Fodder for zombies. You might as well wave a red flag and use smoke signals."

"Actually, I think I'd make a killer impression in this." I grunt as I tug it tighter, forcing the buttons closed. It pinches at the shoulders and pulls at my arms, making me look like a stretched-out toy soldier.

"Right. You're killing the outfit...and my will to live."

I bark out a laugh. "Think you could do better?"

"Obviously."

She wanders over to a rack of gowns and pulls out a glitzy sequin number. Hannah shoots me a quick look over her shoulder. "Can't wait to see the pants that go with your outfit," she says as she disappears into the changing room.

At a nearby rack, I yank out a pair of trousers that are clearly too short. I tug them on over my jeans, the legs stopping halfway up my calves.

A ridiculous figure stares back at me from the mirror, but it only fuels me. Standing in my best pose, I wait for Hannah to emerge. When she does, she's a vision of glitter and tulle, looking every bit like she's ready to accept an award. But the look is spoiled as she doubles over in laughter when she sees me.

"Apocalypse chic." I hold my pose.

She's still smiling at my outfit as she does an exaggerated model turn of her own. "How's this for 'surviving in style'?"

"Yes, *Mad Max* would definitely approve."

"You, on the other hand, not so much."

"Pfftt,.Say no more." I disappear into the fitting room, throwing on a pair of suspenders and an impossibly tight dress shirt, the buttons straining as I step out striking my best 'serious business guy' pose.

Her face lights up in laughter, but she composes herself quickly and makes her way to the dress rack again then strides past me to the change rooms. She emerges in a bright red ball gown that drags along the ground.

"Not bad, but clearly I need something more suitable to match," I dash to grab a sparkly tuxedo shirt with way too many ruffles and pants that were made to be worn by someone four times my size.

When I step out of the dressing room Hannah loses it, her laughter spilling from her more easily now. She picks out a full-length gown with a hoop skirt that gives her about three feet of personal space in every direction.

"Oh, it's on." Sprinting to the racks, I yank out a pair of pants that hug my thighs like shrink-wrap, and a suit jacket that only reaches mid-forearm.

We dart in and out of dressing rooms, each of us emerging faster and more over-the-top than before, barely able to keep up with ourselves.

Finally, we both stagger out, wheezing from laughter. Hannah's in a garish pink dress with a neckline that's practically at her chin and a hem that pools around her feet, while I'm stuck in a too-tight suit that cuts off circulation around my calves, the pants stopping well above my ankles.

Hannah looks at me, stifling a snort. "Well, if you're going for 'regrettable tuxedo choice,' you nailed it."

A grin spread across my face. "Bold words from someone dressed like a cupcake."

"I was going for 'bedazzled lampshade' actually."

"And you've definitely pulled it off."

We both burst into laughter still eyeing one another, amused. It doesn't matter what Hannah is wearing, she looks fucking beautiful, all happy and full of smiles. I'm not sure my tight shirt can conceal my hammering heart.

"Alright, let's get out of here before the mannequins judge us," I say, attempting a formal bow in my absurd outfit.

Hannah curtsies in response, barely managing not to trip over the ridiculous skirt. "Lead the way, Mr. Apocalypse Chic."

"I knew you'd come around," I say and offer her my arm. She hesitates for a split-second before sliding hers into mine.

We strut down the mall like we own the place, both of us dressed like over-the-top characters from an outlandish costume party. And for a moment, the whole strange setup feels worth it just to see her laugh like that, every inch of tension gone between us, even if only for now.

We keep walking along the deserted mall, till we see the jewellery shop. Hannah stops, admiring the pieces behind the glass. She eyes a silver pendant, simple but elegant, shaped like a small leaf. Her stare lingers on the piece.

"See something you like?" I ask, nudging her.

She hesitates, her fingers hovering over the glass. "I... I've wanted this forever."

My gaze flicks from her face to the pendant, "Hannah, you can have anything you want..."

Her large eyes lock onto mine, her expression hardens. "No, I can't." She lets her hand drop from mine, turning away and brushing past me without another glance.

11. Cracks

Ethan

Hannah lazes in a seating pod not far from the camp shop. She's armed with her club and is nose deep in a book. She can use some space, and I can use some time to clear my head.

I walk casually, occasionally glancing over my shoulder as I make my way to the £3 novelty shop - full of knick-knacks and cheap manufactured knock off toys.

It's hidden in the dress up section among the other plastic toys. To the untrained eye it looks like a useless, plastic toy phone, but I know exactly what it is. I walk to the front of the shop scanning the empty mall ensuring Hannah is nowhere to be seen before sneaking to the back, sliding the sim card in and turning the phone on.

I dial the number.

"Hello?" the voice on the other end seems surprised to hear me.

"It's me."

"Obviously, who else would it be?"

"Snarky as always I see, even an apocalypse couldn't cheer you up."

"Well, it cheered me up a little."

I can almost hear the smile in her voice as she takes a long drag on the other end of the phone. "You did an amazing job."

"I know."

"Of course you do." She scoffs on the other end. "How are things on the front?'

"The natives are getting restless."

"Remind them they will be handsomely paid."

"I have been. How is it going?"

"I don't know. One moment she's hot, the other cold. I can't seem to say anything right." I push a breath past clenched teeth, running a hand through my hair. "I don't get women."

Her husky laugh comes through the phone. "Same, babe. Give her food and keep her warm, that usually makes me happy."

"I'll do that, make sure the night shift makes things believable again."

"On it." She hisses as she takes another long drag.

"Hey, do you think I've taken this too far?"

"Waaaaaayyyyy too far. Some might say controlling and obsessive."

"It was your idea!" I'm instantly defensive.

"I didn't say it was wrong... You love that girl, you said you'd do anything, and you did, now stop wasting the time you bought yourself and do what you came to do."

"You're so bossy."

"I love you too."

The line drops out.

A sudden clank has me spinning and shoving the phone

into my back pocket. My heart ricochets around my ribs in a frantic dance. Then I see the culprit—a stuffed teddy whose Velcro has finally let go, tumbling onto the shelf below brimming with remote-controlled cars.

I forget about the phone and reach for one of the cars, its sleek body just waiting for a mission.

I have an idea.

Searching through the aisle I find batteries, a pen and notebook. I tear the plastic away from the notebook and open it up then lean over the counter, carefully scribbling on a piece of paper. The pen scratches across the surface as I write the words slowly, trying to make it as clear as possible. After a moment, I sit back and read it over.

It's simple:

Dinner at the food court? 7PM.

I lean back, admiring my sheer brilliance. Crossing back to the gleaming red car I attach the note with a bit of tape, securing it in a way that she'll notice it immediately. The car's bright red contrasts with the white paper, the note almost too big for it, but it'll work.

Stepping back, I admire my handy work. Simple but effective.

I flick the switch, and the car hums to life, the small wheels whirring in the quiet of the deserted mall. It jerks forward, moving in a wobbly path toward the rest area usually packed with tired husbands having endured their wives shopping trip long enough, now occupied by one stunning woman with a head buried in a book.

She jerks up at the sound, setting the book down and gripping the club in readiness as the mechanical wheeze reverberates through the empty space. Her head swings from side to side till she spots the car heading her way. Hannah scans the area looking for me, but I'm out of sight, well-hidden around the corner.

The little car bumps against the foot of the couch she has taken possession of, and she looks down, a frown on her face. I nudge it forward again, tapping it when she doesn't pick it up right away. She straightens out, finally reaching for the car.

She unfolds the note while I hold my breath, her gaze skimming over the words. Her eyes flick up for a second, sweeping over the store as if wondering where it came from, but she doesn't spot me. I'm still out of view, my pulse races at the base of my throat.

Her fingers tighten around the note, and she stands up slowly, turning in a small circle. Still trying to find me. I stand still, holding my breath, only the rush of blood in my ears breaking the silence.

Her lips press together in that way they do when she's annoyed, but her eyes? They flicker with something warmer. Curiosity, maybe?

Hannah picks up her discarded book and walks off, the note clutched tightly in her hand.

I remain tucked out of sight, a quiet smile tugging at my mouth.

At least I know she got the message.

The rest is up to her.

12. Light Years Away

Ethan

It's not much of a set up; a few scattered candles on deserted tables and cold chicken sandwiches on paper plates with a box of orange juice for each of us.

I sit and wait.

I've changed my ridiculously uncomfortable outfit to a well-fitted suit. I look more than presentable. In fact, if I wasn't so modest I'd go so far as calling myself handsome, but I'm going to leave that up to Hannah.

Footsteps echo from somewhere behind me. I turn and clench my jaw to prevent it from falling to the floor. Looks like I'm not the only one who decided to change.

Hannah walks over. She is wearing an elegant figure-hugging black cocktail dress, inching just over her knees and exposing her shoulders. Her hair is limp and falls across her shoulders, but somewhere she has found some make up and is wearing a subtle lipstick with a touch of eyeliner high-lighting her stunning eyes. I swallow hard, waiting as she saunters over, watching her body move.

"Wow," is all I manage as she looks up and down my body. "Did you go shopping?"

"More like shoplifting..." I chuckle at her humour. "You cleaned up okay too, I guess."

"You guess?"

She shrugs offering me nothing more.

"Shall we?"

I pull out her chair and she slides into it in a fluid motion, gaze flicking to the sandwiches and juice boxes.

"I see you went all out." Hannah reaches for the plastic container.

"Only the best for you, my lady."

She scoffs as I sit down across from her and looks around the deserted food hall. "Was it hard to get a reservation?"

"There was a waiting list... They're probably going to kick us out soon."

Her lips turn in a sweet smile, and she takes a bite of her sandwich. "French?"

"Mmmmm - Poulet à la Crème."

"The *Crème* tastes a lot like mayonnaise." She speaks with her mouth half full.

"It's traditional. An ancient recipe, perfected by sandwich shops everywhere."

"You're so cultured." Her compliment is as tangy as the mayonnaise.

"You have no idea the things I could teach you."

"Like which aisle in the grocery store to pick up this brand?"

"Among other things."

A razor-thin smile cuts across her face, one brow lifting in mock disbelief. "Oh? You know things?"

"At least two."

"Wow, that's a surprise."

"Surprised myself too when I realised."

Hannah giggles. It's sweet and genuine and fills out the empty space, making it feel somehow smaller and warmer. "Must have been hard for you."

"Could be harder."

Her big eyes search my face at the obvious innuendo, and she shifts in her chair, disguising her amusement with another bite.

We fall into a comfortable silence. We can't talk about our parents or our lives. That was all before, none of those things exist anymore.

"So, what are you going to do when we get out of here?" She finally breaks the silence.

"Not sure, maybe go find a beautiful zombie bride and live happily ever after."

"Ethan…"

I sigh, the guilt weighing heavily on me like a rain-soaked blanket. How do you talk about the unknown without getting broken-hearted? I know exactly what I plan on doing when this is all over.

"I don't know, Hannah. What will *you* do?"

"Travel? See the world?"

"That's a good plan."

"Is it?" She looks wistfully at the vacant spaces around us.

"Sure. No lines. No crowds. No entry fees. The whole world to yourself. Paris, Rome, Tokyo. Pick a spot."

She barks a short, incredulous laugh. "And how exactly do I get there? Steal a plane?"

"Why not? I'll fly it for you."

She tilts her head, lips pursed, eyes sparkling with amused scepticism. "You can't even fly."

"Tiny insignificant detail."

She shakes her head, but the smile's already creeping in. "I'll get you a boat."

"We're in the middle of the country."

"You seem to keep coming up with excuses for all my solutions, maybe you just really want to stay here with me."

"Actually, I think the boat sounds like a great idea. Even though you'd probably sink it before we left the car park."

"Ouch."

We exchange a smile.

We eat the rest of dinner in silence, each topic more sensitive than the next; our family, the past, the future...

When we are done, I clear our plates. "Dessert? There's some exotic chocolate mousse in the fridge."

"No thank you. I think I've had all the culture I can handle for one day."

"But it's E X O T I C."

"So is Casu Marzu, but that doesn't mean you should eat it."

"Some people do."

"Maybe they prefer death over spending too much time with you..." she brings her fingers to her chin slowly stroking it as if in deep thought. "On second thought desert does sound great..."

"Mm, turns out the kitchen has just run out."

"What a pity."

"Yeah, It's terrible. Walk you home?"

A faint smile touches her lips, she laces her fingers through mine and stands.

We walk in silence, the sound of her heels hitting tiles echoes in the empty halls. It's the sound of a hammer nailing our coffins shut, ending our future, or at least I imagine that's what Hannah must be hearing. All I hear is a ticking clock reminding me that our time is ending and that I need to work harder to win Hannah back.

Hannah's warm hand is still in mine when we arrive at the camping store and lead her to our makeshift hideaway. She looks stunning, but her face is crestfallen and the humour that clung to her at the beginning of the night has slid away.

Slowing my steps, I glance at her. "What's wrong?" It's better to pretend I don't know.

She lets out a faint, brittle laugh. "It just... it all feels a little pointless... Tomorrow it'll still be this. We'll still be here. Inside. Stuck." She doesn't look at me when she says it; her eyes are fixed somewhere far beyond the shelves.

"Stay here," I say.

"Where else am I going to go?"

I ignore her and make my way to one of the electronic stores. When I get back Hannah is no longer in her dress. It's hanging dutifully on the store hanger, and I know that she will likely return it to its owner ensuring it's still in perfect condition.

"I have something for you."

Her eyes light up as she looks at me.

I set the projector down and walk over to the camping area grabbing a handful of pillows that I place on the floor. "Come sit."

Tentatively Hannah comes to sit at my side and waits.

The projector clicks on.

The ceiling explodes with the night sky, stars and constellations swim across the ceiling. Hannah's face breaks into a wondrous smile. She stares at the display twinkling above us, but my gaze remains on her.

"This is stunning," She's entranced, staring up as the

constellations swirl across her face, her eyes following each flashing light like they might lead her somewhere.

"It is," my voice cracks. I can't drag my stare away from her face. When her eyes finally catch mine, colour rises in her cheeks, and she turns back to the ceiling. I clear my throat, "I just wanted to give you something. Bring a little of the outside in..."

We both gaze at the ceiling as a deep silence engulfs us swallowed by the makeshift universe, scattered above us. It's almost enough to make me forget that we're surrounded by concrete walls and abandoned stores. Almost.

I don't even realise I'm leaning closer until I feel the warmth of her shoulder brushing against mine. I freeze, the heat pooling in my chest. Hannah doesn't flinch away, she doesn't react at all, and I have no idea if she's even aware of this effect she has on me, or if I affect her at all.

Stealing a glance, I take in the way her lashes cast shadows on her cheeks, the slow, steady rise and fall of her breath, the almost imperceptible shiver when our skin touches. Or maybe I imagined that last sensation, but I don't care. I hold on to it as my hand hovers just an inch from hers, I ache to reach across the gap and lace her fingers in mine.

"Look, there's Orion." Her voice shatters the silence and any illusion of intimacy as she points at the famous constellation. "See the belt? Those three stars, in a row."

"Wow, an expert in our midst," I say with mock admiration.

"We can't all be French culinary experts."

"I'll be honest, I don't like Orion's Belt. It's a huge waist of space."

"Terrible joke, three stars." She punches my shoulder in feigned disgust.

"What do you mean? It was stellar!"

"No comet." She rolls her eyes dramatically then turns back to the sky and points elsewhere. "Do you know about the Pleiades?"

"The what?"

"The seven stars, right there." She looks at me with a grin. "They're the Seven Sisters or Wives—depending on which mythology you follow."

"Wow." I'm genuinely awed by Hannah, not just her enthusiasm but her deep knowledge of so many things. I've travelled twice as much, lived a far more privileged lifestyle, yet somehow, she knows far more than I do. "Which mythology do you follow?"

"Well, the Greeks were tragic—seven sisters grieving. Jewish myth is romantic. The Aboriginals say they were young girls, the Baltics made it all about the devil, and the Mono Indians, well I guess you could call them amusing?"

"Amusing how exactly?" I turn to study her face.

"Well, Mono legend has it that the Pleiades are seven wives who loved onions."

"Onions?"

"Yeah, the wives ate wild onions, which angered their husbands who threw them out of their homes. The wives eventually wandered into the sky and became the Pleiades cluster. Now they live happily in 'sky country'."

"Live happily?"

"Sure, no men around to tell them what they should or shouldn't eat." She laughs, pink staining her cheeks.

"But seriously? Onions!"

"Could be worse."

"How?"

"Anchovies? Now that's a crime against humanity."

"True. That's the kind of thing you get exiled for in *all* cultures." She giggles at my lame joke. "What else you got?"

She points to another area above us. "That's Andromeda. The chained princess."

"Didn't really think the stars were this kinky."

"If you want kink, you can always turn to Uranus." She's smiling, her eyes glinting with mischief. I know there's something hidden behind that look.

"Uranus? Everyone knows Earth can fit into it like 63 times." I shot off the only fact I know.

She turns to face me, her face serious. "64 if it just relaxed."

We both burst into laughter, she falls back, her head on my shoulder and, for a brief moment, we are our old selves, laughing and comfortable and finding joy even in the darkest moments. My heart pricks at her touch and the sound of her laugh.

She glances over at me, her expression easing for the briefest moment. Her laughter falters as I take her in, unable to muster the will to look away.

I turn to her fully, barely breathing, caught somewhere between anticipation and the feeling of falling without a safety net.

Her gaze locks on mine and her lips part slightly, her breath hitching.

A shiver ripples down my spine.

Hannah doesn't pull back. If anything, she leans in just the slightest of inches, and every nerve in my body hums with electricity.

I lean in, hope and desire smashing in my chest, but as I do, she turns, inhaling deeply, as if she is coming to her senses, returning to reality. I'm flooded with a wave of cold disappointment suspended somewhere between what could've been and whatever we just created instead.

Her gaze returns to the night sky. "I think I better go to sleep." She gets up, steps away and back towards our hide-out. She stops for a second and looks back. "Thanks, for this."

All I can do is meet her gaze, my throat too clogged with emotion, my lungs empty of air, my body charged and aching with a need too desperate for her.

"Good night," she whispers as she slinks into the room' leaving me alone with the starry night. I search for a while, but I find no shooting stars.

13. You don't need zombies
for your world to end

12/01/2010

Hannah

I keep reminding myself that this isn't the worst idea ever. Dinner with Ethan's mother is a step closer to us being real, to our relationship being more than a secret dream shared only by the two of us. Still, as he parks the car and the engine dies outside his massive mansion, the nerves eat away at my skin.

The door closes behind us with a dull thud, and I'm instantly hit with the overwhelming scent of fresh flowers, polished wood, and something slightly too strong, almost clinical. It's the smell of wealth—expensive, cold, and a little intimidating. My hands run down my dress, ironing out the creases. I already feel underdressed and out of my depth and we've only crossed the threshold.

Ethan leads me through the grand hallway. "Relax, Hannah," he says with a gentle smile, trying to be reassuring, though his tone is clipped and laced with nervousness. "It's just dinner."

"Yup. Yes," I correct almost automatically, "fully relaxed."

Everyone in the town knows that the Vale family is wealthy, though standing here now and taking it all in, the description no longer fits. Wealthy seems too poor a word—their fortune is immense—innumerable, but there's a difference between knowing it and seeing it. Everything around me is sharp, meticulous and worth more than I can dream of earning in a lifetime.

His mother waits for us at the dinner table. She is the epitome of a rich bitch, the benchmark for every stereotype out there—overly made up, hiding her ageing face, over-priced branded clothes, the required pearl necklace and flawless nails.

She screams perfection, not a hair out of place, neat and untouched like her house. Everything about her is surface, everything immaculate under the scrutiny of strangers.

Standing up as we enter, she reaches her son. "Ethan, darling." Her voice drips with exaggerated adulation as she kisses both cheeks, smiling, her fake veneers glinting underneath the chandelier.

"Mother." He returns the gesture and takes a small step backwards. "Where is Dad?"

"He was called out last minute. You know how it is."

His face tightens for a second and his nod is nearly imperceptible. He turns his attention back to me, the tension in his features melting away. "This is Hannah." He smiles at the mention of my name, and a warmth spreads through me.

Marjorie Vale turns towards me, her cold eyes running up and down my body, taking in every inch. Her gaze lingers on my Primart bought dress and makes my stomach churn. It's not an overt judgment, but it's there, like she's already measuring me for what I lack.

"Hannah, what a... unique choice in attire," she comments, her smile tight. "Welcome to my humble abode." She shakes my hand weakly, her hands as cold as the blasting air con.

I force a smile, the urge to respond rises, but I don't, because what would I even say? Ethan's hand lands in mine and squeezes, a silent reassurance. He leads me to the table —which could easily sit twenty people—and we all take our place. It's set perfectly; everything gleams beneath the hush of the chandelier light. This place is more like a palace than a home. I'm not sure how to sit, how to act. All my nerves curl in my gut and squeeze in a tight ball.

"So, darling, tell me everything. Where did you meet... her?" She's already forgotten my name or making sure I know she is trying to.

"I've told you about Hannah, Mother. I've known her since I was ten years old."

Her stare snaps back to me, as if I'm some sort of rare animal she's never seen before. "Ah, your *little friend*." She brushes him off, laughing to herself. Ethan squeezes my hand again under the table.

A server walks in dressed like an uptight penguin and pours wine into our glasses. Tension hangs in the silent air as he does.

"So, Anna—"

"It's Hannah." Ethan corrects her before she continues.

"Yes, of course." But she doesn't correct herself. "So, you go to school?"

"Yes, I'll be going to Uni next year."

His mother purses her lips as if I used a swear word, "*Uni.*"

"University, Kent."

"Ah, how quaint." She tips the wine to her mouth and takes a large sip.

"They have a great program there." I sound defensive.

"Oh? What are you planning to study?" Her voice is syrupy sweet, almost as if she's interested, but she's anything but.

"She wants to be a teacher." Ethan's voice is laced with pride as he tells his mother.

"I want to make a difference. It's important to me. Shaping the minds of future generations."

"Shaping to be more ambitious, I hope." The jab is subtle but unmistakable.

"Mother," Ethan's voice is a little firmer now. "There's nothing wrong with wanting to shape the future. Not everything's about the bottom line."

"No, it isn't darling, you are right, but it will be when you are running your father's company." She stares at me when she speaks to him, like she's already decided I'm here to line my own pockets, not change the world.

I force a smile. "I like helping people, and that's enough for me."

"Of course it would be."

The subtle insult stings more than it should, but Ethan doesn't miss a beat. He looks directly at his mother, his voice sharp and biting. "That's enough. I don't appreciate you speaking about Hannah like that."

His words hang in the air, unexpected but appreciated. His mother's eyes flash for a moment, surprise quickly masked by an icy veil.

"I'm just pointing out the obvious," she says, as if she's done nothing wrong. "It's just that people with dreams like hers tend to get lost along the way. So much potential wasted on something as... *modest* as teaching."

Ethan leans forward, his tone no longer polite but firm. "There's nothing wrong with wanting to help others, Mother. And you need to start respecting that."

Before she can say anything else our food arrives.

"Thank you." She smiles at her house staff, almost too sweetly, as if the last few minutes didn't happen at all. "Please, help yourselves."

The food is exquisite. Delicate cuts of steak, some kind of truffle pasta, and wine that probably costs more than I make in a month, maybe a year. But it all tastes sour, tainted by her clear disdain.

Dinner continues. His mother all but ignores my existence, speaking only to her son about his father and the multitude of business deals he has been dealing with.

Ethan's eyes glaze over as he half listens and his hand drifts down to mine every so often squeezing, reminding me that I'm still here, that I am still important.

To him.

When dinner finally ends, his mother stands. "We will enjoy after dinner drinks in the lounge."

I clear my throat, nervous tension dancing under my skin. "I need to use the loo please."

"Thank you for the announcement, dear. Darling, won't you show her the way?" Without much more she glides out of the room.

"Ignore her," Ethan says with his hand on my back, guiding me out of the room.

"She's impossible to ignore."

"She's all bite, no bark." He tries to reassure me as we walk down a long corridor.

"But she's so..."

"I know. I'm sorry. She's always been like this, but you have to know, I'm nothing like her. Please don't think her behaviour defines me, or us."

"Of course you are nothing like her," I say, forcing a smile. "But still...."

Ethan's jaw tightens as if he's biting back something more. "Don't let her do this. She doesn't know you. She doesn't know us. But I promise you that I'll make sure she never makes you feel like you're not enough."

"Ethan, I—"

"—Don't. Don't apologise for her, please," his eyes search mine. "You don't have to prove anything. I don't care about her opinion. It's yours that matters to me."

I glance down, suddenly self-conscious under his gaze. "But you have to care what she thinks."

"Why? She's not the one I want to spend the rest of my life with." His words steal any further protest. Ethan bends towards me, sealing his words with a stolen kiss. "I love you, Hannah Jones," he whispers into my ear and pulls me into a tight hug.

His reassurance uncoils some of my tension, and I melt against him.

He releases his hold on me though I am loath that he does. "You better go before she starts getting the wrong idea. Once you are done it's the ninth door on the left."

"The ninth, hey?"

He shrugs. "I could leave you a map, but I trust your counting."

"Famous last words." I jab at his ribs, and he steps back, turning away with a gentle smile.

The bathroom is just as lavish as the rest of the home. Gleaming marble floors and walls in muted hues of cream and gold. The vanity is an expanse of polished wood with gold fixtures, while a rain shower encased in glass boasts intricate mosaic tiles. Every detail, from the plush monogrammed towels to the scented candles, whispers indulgence and opulence. Guilt pricks at me when I dry my hands and defile the perfection of the space. Then I rush out of the room and start counting doors.

Stepping back into the hallway, I count under my breath. "Five... six..."

The floor beneath my feet is the same pale marble, tempered by a deep navy runner rug that stretches the length of the corridor, with gold thread worked into swirling patterns.

"Seven..."

Framed paintings hang between each door, all original, no doubt. Oil portraits with moody lighting—likely chosen by his mother—and abstract landscapes. Their worth is unimaginable.

"Eight..."

A narrow console table sits against the wall, topped with a silver tray of decanters, crystal, of course, and a small vase of orchids so white they almost look artificial.

"Nine."

I stop.

Their voices drift through the open door and I lean against the wall, listening. I know I shouldn't, but the temptation compels me. I just need a few more minutes to steel myself. His mother has already made me feel more than insignificant.

"No."

"I'm not asking you, I'm telling you." Ethan's voice carries through the doorway.

"Ha," Marjorie's tone curdles the air, sharp and unkind. The sound sends shivers down my spine. Her disdain seeps through the wall and sticks to my skin. "That girl doesn't belong with our kind."

"What kind? Human?"

"No, Darling, civilised."

"Mum!"

"Not *Mum*, did you see what she was wearing?"

"She did her best."

"Well frankly her best is mediocre."

"I think she looks beautiful."

"That's because you are leaving the thinking to the wrong body part."

"Seriously..."

"Seriously? Yes, darling, let's be serious. How do you think this is going to play out exactly? You will go off to Oxford and she will be off to wherever—"

"—Kent."

His interruption doesn't stop her. "It's not Oxford or Yale, is it? Think, Ethan. It's nonsense. You know none of this makes sense. Best thing you can do is meet someone more suited to your... calibre."

"I love her."

"That's wonderful, dear, that's important, love is a good thing. But love won't feed you or educate you. It won't open doors and give you a future. Love is for stories and fairytales, and you, son, live in the real world."

"But—"

"And I'm sure given time you will fall in love with another girl who's just as pretty and smart but has more to offer."

"More to offer?"

"Yes, dear, quality of life."

"Mum! I will not stand here and let you talk about Hannah like that. She is not some girl living on the streets, she is beautiful and intelligent and has plans. She wants to go to university—"

"—Yes, yes to be a wonderful teacher." The word curls off her tongue with such contempt as if the whole concept of education offends her. "How noble, and how totally unambitious."

"Mum, stop."

"No, you stop. Stop living in some romanticised notion in your head and come back to reality. You cannot marry that girl. She doesn't belong. She will tarnish the Vale name, and how embarrassing to have her on your arm at functions explaining to people she's a school teacher. You've had your fun, dipped your member into the slums, sewn your wild oats and whatnot, now break up with her and let's forget this whole chapter happened."

"How dare you talk about her like that? She is the love of my life, and I will marry her, and there is nothing you or Dad can do about it."

"You're right, dear, there is nothing at all we can do about it, it's your life—and likely to be a long one—so you get to choose its trajectory. You can walk out of this room, chase after your love, and settle for scraping by on barely enough income with nothing but hope to keep you warm. Love doesn't pay the bills, nor does it put food on the table or clothes on your back. You'll shoulder all the costs yourself, since neither your father nor I will lift a finger to help. Your accounts will be frozen, your inheritance gone. You'll end up like the rest of the plebs in this town working for your father, owing us everything. Or... you come to your senses and accept the path laid out for you. You'll be leaving for Oxford in six weeks."

"Hannah is not a pleb."

"If you say so, dear, feel free to go find her."

She makes it sound like a death sentence. Like loving me is the dumbest, most self-destructive thing her son could do.

Like I'm nothing.

She steps out, notices me, and a smile creeps along her face, slow and knowing, half pity, half self-satisfaction, like she's just won. And as I peer into the room and see Ethan's back, his shoulders hunched and head down, it's clear that she has.

His voice reaches me before I see him. It's ragged and loud, like he's been running. I don't answer.

I keep sitting, letting the old swing creak beneath me as my feet push against the gravel. Wind tugs at my dress and my knuckles whiten as I grip the chain. I wish I could forget what I overheard.

But I can't.

I had no idea she despised me so deeply, without even knowing me. Her words were so cold, so measured, so final they're seared into me. To her I'm an annoying smudge on her perfect stained-glass windows, something that needs to be wiped away.

"Hannah?"

I stay silent. He steps closer.

"Hannah." He says my name again, softer this time, like maybe if he says it right, he can undo everything. I dig my heels in and let the swing still. A tremor runs through my ribs; my throat locks, air snagging on the way out.

I don't look up.

"Why did you leave? I've been looking everywhere."

"Should've just asked your mother where the plebs go."

He flinches but his face shifts, understanding dawning behind his eyes. "You heard that."

"I heard everything."

He lets out a slow breath. "She doesn't matter. She can say whatever she wants. I love you."

I look at him now, really look. "And then what? We pretend none of it matters? Pretend she didn't say I'd be the reason you end up broke and useless and working some dead-end job just like the rest of the town?"

He opens his mouth, but I cut him off.

"Your parents seem pretty confident you'd choose money over me."

"They're wrong."

"Are they? Because—"

"Stop, please. Just let me..." He rakes his fingers through his hair. "We can come up with a solution, something to protect both you and the family assets."

"Right..."

"It's complicated." He falters.

"It's really not." I smooth my dress, the cheap one from Primart his mother *had* to point out as not good enough. "You either love me more than money or you don't. Your mother made her position clear, now I need to know yours."

"That's not fair."

"Fair?" I laugh, but it's sharp and humourless.

"It doesn't matter," he insists. "I want to marry you, Hannah, grow old with you." He coaxes my hand off the chain and folds it in his. "All we have to do is keep it quiet, just for a while. Just until things settle. We don't have to tell anyone."

I snatch my hand back and glare at him. "So that's what I am to you? I get to be your dirty little secret? Your shame? I'm not interested in a love that lives in the shadows."

"It's not like that."

"It's exactly like that." I stand. "You won't stand up to her. You won't stand up for me."

"Hannah, I'm trying to protect you." His voice leaks desperation. "If I walk away from everything, we'll have nothing. No future. You don't understand what money can do, how far it can get us..."

"Don't stand there and tell me I don't understand money or family because I do. My family might not be as rich as yours, but we get by, we're happy. I'm not willing to be erased just because you want both. Your life and my love. You can't have both, Ethan. Not if you're too scared to name one out loud."

"It's not like that..." He sounds like a song stuck on repeat.

"Fine. Let's get married, tomorrow, next week. Tell her. Tell everyone."

He opens his mouth, then closes it. The silence that follows cuts deeper than anything he could have said.

It lands like a slap, hot and stinging.

"Right, that's what I thought." The words a bitter sound.

He reaches for me, desperate now. "You don't understand, Ha—"

"Because I'm just your *little, poorly dressed, will-not-attend-an-ivy-league-school friend*, right?" My voice splinters. "A replaceable background extra in your perfect life."

"That's not what I meant—"

"But it's what you said."

He swallows, and there's a flash of regret in his eyes. But I'm already walking. Not fast. Just steady.

Away.

He doesn't follow.

And that, more than anything, is my answer.

14. Day 3

04/11/2025

Ethan

I'm giddy as I approach the £3 shop for my daily check-in. Over breakfast Hannah gave me looks. Not her snarky cold stares but sweet looks with her eyelashes fluttering. The ice between us has finally melted. It's a live wire running under my skin and suddenly the ember that has been dimmed inside of me has sparked into life with renewed hope. And maybe it's dangerous but still, I sense the intensity between us and for the first time I know she feels it too.

She's gone off to wash herself in a basin somewhere and I've slipped back into the shop. I reach for the phone.

'Where the hell are you? We have a problem.'

That is not the message I want to see as I power up the cell. *'What's wrong?'* My fingers fly over the keys.

'We have intruders, they've made it past the barriers, they'll be at the doors in five minutes.'

'What?? Stop them!' A jolt punches through me, I've

come too far to have everything fall apart just as it's starting to come together.

'*We tried.*'

I drag my hand along my face letting out a frustrated breath. '*They can't come inside.*'

'*I know.*'

'*If they try, you'll have to do something.*'

'*Like what?*'

'*Rob will have to bite them.*'

'*Are you crazy?*'

'*Maybe.*'

Three bubbles appear on my screen then vanish. I stare at the screen. Heat flashes up my neck and my skin prickles. The dots reappear.

'*Rob says he won't do it.*'

'*I'll pay him extra.*'

'*What if they have rabies?*'

'*It's a chance I'm willing to take!!!!*'

Three more dots appear on the screen but it's too late as I hear my name echoing down the empty hallways. I run out of the shop and towards her voice.

"Ethan, Ethan come quick." I rush towards the front doors where we both watch the intruders. Of course Hannah doesn't see them as that—she sees them as survivors.

A family hurries towards the mall, glancing over their shoulders. Behind them, the zombies shuffle closer, slower but relentless.

The man is casually dressed in a polo and jeans, but his wife and teenage daughter are made up to the nines. The wife is wearing a summer dress, heels, and not a hair is out of place, while the daughter's eyelashes could be seen from the moon, her crop top clings to her chest and her shorts hang too low. She is covered in brand names and too much make-up. They do not look like survivors; they look like they've stepped out of a glossy magazine and have headed to the mall for a family day.

Disaster.

I don't know what Hannah is taking in, but the family reaches the doors and sees us on the other side of the glass. They keep looking over their shoulders as the zombies close the distance at an agonisingly slow speed. I know they are keeping to character but the tension's a live monster under my skin; my pulse hammers at my throat like it's searching for a way out.

The man tries the doors just to find them locked and barricaded. He knocks, making eye contact with me. I shake my head and he frowns, seemingly unhappy with my response.

The zombies close in, and the wife says something, panic now drawn along her face. The man turns around and his demeanour changes. The family bangs on the glass doors, with each fist smashing against the glass panels they become more desperate.

Hannah moves, eyes fixed on them. "Ethan, we have to let them in."

A cold weight slides down my spine. I put a hand out to stop her. "We can't."

She shrugs my hand away and glares at me, disbelief flickering across her face. "They're alive! Look at them!"

The woman outside is shouting now, her words unintelligible through the thick glass. Her hands pressed against the glass, eyes pleading. Her head keeps flicking over her shoulder. The teenager has lost her facade of being cool, calm and collected, and she clings to her mother's arm screaming and battering the glass. The man's fists pound harder, the sound echoing through the empty mall like a drumbeat of panic.

"Ethan!"

I force myself to stay calm. "We don't know if it's safe."

Hannah rushes forward, ignoring my concerns, already pulling at the items we carefully arranged to keep everything out. "Help me!"

Reluctantly, I join her, but my movements are slow, deliberate. The wood barely shifts. The barricade holds.

The zombies are closing in, their groans louder now. Rob, with his makeup more grotesque than most, tattered clothing giving him an air of decay, leads the pack. His eyes lock on mine. Even beneath the costume, the message is clear: *I hate you.*

I hope he sees the desperation in my eyes, the apology. Technically, this isn't *my* fault; they should have never come through the town limit to begin with.

The man outside slams his palm against the glass one last time. A scream tears from the woman's throat as the zombies reach them.

Rob grabs the man, his eyes lock onto mine just once more as if asking me if this is what I really want. The subtle tilt of my head is enough to give him the green light. Rob's teeth sink into the man's shoulder. Blood stains his shirt almost instantly, an amount too large to comprehend unless Rob pierced a major artery.

Hannah gasps, hand flying to her mouth, eyes wide in horror. The teenager's cries are muffled as more figures close in on the family and drag them away, disappearing around the corner.

Hannah's voice trembles. "Oh my God... They—"

"We can't help them now," I Say, my voice low. "They're bitten. We don't know how the virus spreads."

She stares at me, tears welling. "You... You just let them die."

I don't answer. The truth settles like a stone in my gut.

Hannah pushes me away then frantically begins to push at our barricade, sending chairs, trolleys, and plant bases flying, attempting to reach the door.

"Hannah, stop!" She ignores me.

I reach out and grab her wrist, turning her to me, her teary eyes lock onto mine. "Hannah, it's too late, there's nothing we can do for them."

She wrenches her wrist from my grip. "You just let them die."

"No, I didn't, there was no way we could have saved them."

"Maybe if we —"

"Not even then."

She pushes me away again, this time with less force. I don't move, my feet planted firmly on the ground. Her small fists beat into me as tears fall down her cheeks, her wails coming in raw and desperate. Heat surges under my skin like an electric current as guilt and sadness tear at each other inside me.

Then she's on me, clinging, her sobs tearing out of her, feral and broken. Her entire body shudders against mine, and I hold her. Pulling her closer.

"I didn't know it would feel like this," she whispers, her voice wrecked. "I didn't know watching someone die would feel like being ripped in half."

There's nothing I can say to fix this. She's not just grieving the family outside the door; she's grieving the fracture in the fragile world she's clinging to. I want to promise her it'll be okay, but the only thing I have is the truth, and that's the one thing I can't give her. Not now. I stay quiet, my arms tightening around her and that has to be enough.

"They looked so normal." Her voice breaks. "Like people I'd pass on the street. People who had homes. Lives. Like Laura, like Rob, like everyone. And we just... we let them die." Her breath trembles against my chest, tears soaking through my shirt. She pulls back slightly, her eyes red, unfocused. "We didn't even try."

"We couldn't..."

"Yes, I get it, I know." She presses the heel of her hand to her forehead like she can shove the thoughts back in. "I know we couldn't save them. I know. But knowing doesn't make it feel any better. Like less of a failure. We failed them."

Her knees buckle a little, and I guide us to the floor, sitting down against the wall, pulling her into my lap. She latches on to me like I'm the last solid thing left.

Slowly, her sobs settle, replaced by a quiet that speaks of surrender and acceptance. She pulls back just enough to meet my eyes. Her own still glistening with unshed tears. "Is this what it is now? Watching people die because it's not convenient to help them?"

A tight spike lances my core. "That's not what ha—"

"I don't know how we keep doing this," she cuts me off, her voice fragile but firm. "How we keep pretending there's a tomorrow when all I see is the end, like it's all for nothing."

I swallow. "It's not the end. It's not for nothing." She doesn't understand yet and right now, I don't know how to help her.

She nuzzles into me. "I'm scared."

"I know, but I'll get us through this, to the other side."

"Is there an other side to this?"

"There is, and it's perfect." My pulse ratchets up and the guilt solidifies inside me.

Hannah pulls away, her jaw tightening, resolve flickering in her eyes. She wipes a hand across her face, taking away the tears and shoving her messy hair behind her ears. She looks broken and dishevelled and so very fucking beautiful.

"I need a drink."

I stand up, pulling her up with me. "Follow me."

I push the heavy door aside and I'm greeted with the scent of stale beer and aged wood. The interior is dim; the only lights are the green exit signs above the doors. They reflect off brass fixtures and dark mahogany.

A row of empty barstools line a long counter, their leather cracked and worn. Booths with green velvet cushions sit against the walls, some torn, stuffing peeking through. A dusty jukebox stands silent in the corner.

I notice her eyes lingering on the bottles, her shoulders still tense from the scene outside. Without a word, she crosses the room, sliding behind the bar. Her fingers trail over the labels until she grabs a bottle of whiskey, her movements sharp, deliberate.

"Any preference?" she asks, her voice tight, eyes avoiding mine.

I shake my head. "Whatever works."

She pulls down a couple of glasses and opens a bottle, and she pours. No hesitation, no measuring. The liquid glugs heavily into each glass, almost to the brim.

She slides one toward me, then raises hers, eyes hard. "To survival. Or whatever this is."

I pick up the glass, watching her. "Hannah..."

"Don't." She brings the whiskey to her lips and takes a long, steady sip, barely flinching at the burn. The silence stretches between us, heavy with everything unsaid.

I sip mine, the fire spreading through me. "You can't blame yourself."

Her eyes flash. "I don't. I blame you." She sets the glass down with a hard clink. "They were right there, Ethan. We could've helped."

"We didn't know—"

"We didn't try." Her voice cracks. She looks away, swallowing hard. "I just need a minute."

I watch her, wanting to reach out, but knowing better. She pours herself another drink, her hands trembling slightly as she lifts the glass. Silence settles between us, thick and unyielding.

I swirl the whiskey, watching her. "It could be worse."

She glares at me, arms crossed. "Worse? How, Ethan?"

I raise an eyebrow. "Imagine if it was... giant spiders. Everywhere. And they're smart. They'd set traps."

Her eyes narrow, but there's a flicker of curiosity. "Spiders?"

My mouth twists in a grim smile. "Webs across every doorway, every hallway. You wouldn't hear them coming, just feel those eight legs crawling up your back."

She shudders involuntarily, trying to hide it. "Spiders don't moan like zombies."

"Exactly. Silent. Sneaky. And worst of all? They'd hide in your shoes."

Her lips twitch, but she fights the smile. "You're an idiot."

I shrug, raising my glass. "Better than being spider food."

"Spiders can be killed."

"Fine, what's worse than spiders?"

"A screwpocalypse."

My eyebrows wiggle up and down. "That sounds great, I would totally be up for that."

"No, you idiot, a screwpocalypse. Screws. Gone. Vanished. I mean, literally everything would fall apart."

I raise an eyebrow. "Screws? Not the other thing?"

She rolls her eyes. "Imagine it. Houses, high-rises, all collapsing because those little metal bits hold everything together. Appliances? Dead. Power lines fall, probably electrocuting half the population or starting fires. Cars? Useless. You'd have to walk everywhere or maybe find a horse."

"A horse?"

She ignores me and continues. "Imagine you wear glasses—they've got tiny screws too. So you can't see, you get lost, and, boom, trip over a fallen street sign that used to be upright."

I can't help but grin. "Contacts?"

"You ran out..." She leans forward, animated. "You finally stumble to your crappy job. Limping, obviously, cause of the tumble you took, the elevator's busted and you can't clock in, cause all the computers are in pieces. No power—which is okay cause the building is basically rubble. The poor secretaries are running around with candles, duct-taping everything together."

I laugh, but she's not done.

"You leave, exhausted—not because you worked—but because you spent the day chasing the secretaries with the duct tape. You try to take the bus—cause your horse ran off —but nope. Everything's broken. You pass a grocery store, collapsed. Think you'll grab some spaghetti? That sounds great, you dig through the rubble till you find a pack. But when you get home, it of course lies in a pile too. You find your pot but the handles fall off. Why? Screws. By now, you're tired, hungry, unemployed, and your house is in ruins."

I raise my glass. "I mean..."

She gives a dark, sarcastic smile. "It's bleak. Civilization as we know it has fallen to pieces—literally—no networks or communications, no electricity, the very basic things we take for granted have dissolved into piles of nothing. With no hope, you decide to end it all. You grab a pocketknife, ready to do the deed but... it falls apart. Because it's held together with motherf—"

"Screws..." I finish for her.

She stops, eyes meeting mine, a spark of humour lightening the tension in her gaze as she lifts her now half-empty glass. "Screws, Ethan. The real apocalypse."

"If I had a hat I'd take it off."

"A minute ago, you were wanting to take your pants off instead."

"Is that still an option?"

Her eyes catch mine and, for the tiniest of moment, I swear I can see her considering my request. Instead of answering, she elbows me, and we burst into nervous laughter before she drains her glass.

"Refill?" She tilts her glass towards me, and I grab the bottle, topping up her empty glass.

***

Hannah's weight leans heavily into me as we stumble back toward our little corner in the camping store. Her arm is draped over my shoulders, and I've got one hand gripping her waist, the other holding her wrist to keep her steady.

She's giggling quietly, at what, I'm not even sure anymore. Her words slur just enough to tell me the few drinks she had hit her hard.

"Careful," I murmur, as her foot catches on the edge of a display shelf. I steady her, ignoring the way my pulse jumps at the feel of her pressed so closely against me.

"Mm fine," she mutters, but her head falls against my shoulder like she's testing just how much I'll hold her up. Spoiler alert: it's a lot.

By the time we make it to the air mattress, I'm practically carrying her. We tumble onto the mattress together, not particularly graceful, but it doesn't seem to bother her. She flops onto her side, one arm sliding across my torso as though it's the most natural thing in the world.

I freeze, my breath catching as she snuggles closer, her face nuzzling into my shoulder. The faint scent of her shampoo, something floral, mixes with the warmth of her skin. My muscles seize with sudden awareness, and for a moment, I don't know where to put my hands.

She murmurs something unintelligible and sighs deeply, her entire body melting into mine. It's both exhilarating and terrifying. I want to stay like this forever, and yet I'm hyper-aware of every inch of her pressed against me.

"Ethan," she whispers, her voice barely audible.

"Yeah?"

Nothing. She's already drifting off, her breath evening out. I stare up at the ceiling, willing myself to calm down, but her weight on me is the sweetest kind of torture.

15. The Edge of Knowing

Ethan

I wake with a sharp headache, my throat dry and scratchy as if I swallowed sandpaper. The fluorescent emergency lights in the room feel like they're drilling into my skull.

I glance over at the empty space next to me. Hannah's nowhere in sight. She's probably off somewhere, figuring out her own thoughts. I wonder if she's piecing things together. I'm sure she is. But I can't afford to tell her. Not yet. Distraction is key.

I push myself up from the mattress, trying to quiet the dizziness. It's late evening now. I know that much. The tiny sliver of light from the corner of the room where the last of the sun is dying only highlights that we had managed to drink an entire day away.

I blink and wince. My thoughts feel shredded splintering inside my skull.

I find her by the food court, sitting at one of the tables, a vacant stare on her face as she watches the empty mall. She looks smaller than usual, her shoulders drawn inward, and for a second, I almost regret everything.

But the guilt only lasts a moment before I remind myself this is all part of the plan.

"Hey," forcing a casual tone as I walk up to her. "How're you feeling?"

She looks up at me, her expression tired but thoughtful. "Like I've been hit by a truck." She shifts, wiping her face with the back of her hand. There's a flicker of something else in her eyes. A look she's had since this morning, uneasy, like she's realising things she doesn't quite understand yet.

"I feel that," I mutter, sitting across from her. A part of me wants to make a lame joke, another knows this isn't the right moment.

"I don't get it," Her voice trembles, each word laced with doubt. "It doesn't make sense. I keep thinking it's all a dream, but the longer this goes on, the more... *real* it feels. Everything's messed up, and I don't know how to fix it."

I look at her again, this time really looking, not just seeing the surface. Her face is pale, her features sharper under the dim light, and I want so badly to tell her everything's going to be fine, to give her the comfort she craves. I take a deep breath, watching her closely. Guilt curls through me like icy fingers as I nod along.

"I know," My voice catches. "I don't know how to fix it either." Lies. "But we'll figure it out. Together."

A ragged breath escapes her, part resignation, part disbelief, and her eyes drift to that far away place inside her own thoughts. "How did we end up here?" Her question hangs between us like an accusation. "We're just... *here*. Like this is some weird... illusion. It's just an impossible coincidence, right?"

I know she's not asking for answers, but that doesn't stop

the guilt that rises like acid inside me as she questions everything.

I want to reach for her hand, to show her that I'm here, but I hold back. There's still so much between us, so many things I haven't told her. Like the truth...

"I don't know." Her eyes search mine for some hint of clarity. I hate seeing her like this, so uncertain, so vulnerable.

She shakes her head slightly. "I keep thinking we're going to wake up and it'll all be over. That maybe... This is all just a test or a dream. But you act like it's normal. Like... it's not weird that three people were dragged away by a fucking horde of zombies."

I wince inwardly, but I keep my expression neutral. This is the moment I've been dreading, the moment when she starts figuring it out. She's close. I know it.

"It's not that I think it's normal, it's anything but," I shoot back, a little sharper than I intend. "But freaking out isn't going to help. We need to keep going. If we keep going, we'll get through it."

There's silence again. She looks down at the floor, almost like she's trying to will the whole situation away.

"Yeah. I guess you're right." She pauses, then adds in a low, hesitant tone, "I just wish... I don't know. I just wish I understood what's going on. I keep asking myself if this is real."

I swallow hard, the weight of the lie heavier than ever.

"Sometimes, you don't need to understand everything," I reply. "You just need to keep moving forward."

It's a weak answer, but it's the only one I can give. I can't tell her the truth. Not yet.

She straightens a little squaring her shoulders. "So we figure it out then?"

I lean in towards her, barely a breath between us now. "Yeah," I whisper. "Together."

"Can we get some food first?" Her smile is weak and sad, but the hope is back in her eyes and for now, that's enough for me.

16. Day 4

The morning after the alcohol-fuelled haze, I wake up to silence.

It's not the eerie, suffocating silence of our first days here, the kind that made the mall feel like a tomb. It's something gentler now. Like the world outside doesn't matter as much as the space we've carved for ourselves in here. Like we're settling in. Like it's just the two of us.

Hannah is still asleep beside me, curled up beneath the blanket we scavenged from a homewares store. Her hair is a mess, a few strands falling over her face, and for a second, I just watch her. I shouldn't. I should get up, move around, do something useful.

But I don't.

Because I don't want to.

The shift between us has been happening for days now, slow, creeping, inevitable. Just as I'd hoped.

There's no one else here. No distractions. No rules. Just

her and me, orbiting each other, pulled closer by the history we've shared, the history that was never lost.

She stirs, and moves against me, stilling for a second as she feels the intruder that has joined us in the bed. She's frozen for a second then slides away making space between us. I should apologise, but won't. I want her to know what she does to me, how she makes me feel.

In true Hannah form she ignores the obvious and when she speaks, her voice is thick with sleep. "Morning."

I roll away from her and sit on the edge of the mattress, willing my body to relax. "Technically, it's past noon." I help her break the tension.

She groans, stretching out with a wince. "Feels like morning."

We get up slowly, lazily, like it's a regular Sunday morning and the world is still spinning on its regular axis.

She shuffles over to the bottled water stash, grumbling something under her breath when the cap's on too tight. I take it from her without asking, twist it open in one smooth motion, and get a *look* for my trouble.

"Thanks," she says, but it sounds like she's debating whether or not to kick me in the shin.

"Don't mention it," My reply earns me the tiniest eye roll.

"Wasn't planning to." I return the eye roll as she takes a long sip.

She grabs her toiletry bag—which, I make a mental note —she is yet to thank me for, and we tentatively open the door, making our way towards the hallways. At the door of the camping store we stop, listen, and peek at the large doors.

"Still dead out there?"

She shoots me a look over her shoulder. "Funny."

I let out a long, deliberate breath. "Any movement?"

"Nothing." Her voice is low.

We step into the hall, and I notice her checking again, the uncertainty never leaving her and the fear still there, on the surface, despite all my reassurances, despite the safety of this inner world we have built.

She disappears into the women's bathroom, and I step into the men's, running water over my face. I catch my reflection in the mirror, examining the lines of tension I didn't realise I still carried, and I give myself a small, private smile. Last night plays over in my mind, carrying her back to the mattress, how she pressed into me without realising, the faint warmth of her hand sliding along my chest as she curled into sleep. I splash water over my face again, trying to cool down my thoughts, my body.

I dry my face, trying not to let my thoughts spiral.

Stick to the plan.

I repeat the mantra in my head as I step out of the bathroom. Hannah comes out a minute later and I follow.

She leads us toward the barricade and examines it, running her hand along the bent edge of a trolley, eyes fixed on the gap she'd made yesterday. Chairs still sit off to the side where she'd tossed them, and one of the potted plants has been knocked over, soil spilled in a dark crescent on the floor.

"I messed it up," she whispers, almost to herself.

"You were trying to help them." I step in beside her, lifting the nearest chair and slotting its leg back into the frame. Her eyes dart away from mine, but I see the emotion there, the gratitude. I understand and maybe that's all she needs.

Hannah pushes a trolley, slotting it back into place. I press it forward, the scrape of metal against tile echoing through the empty concourse. Our hands meet briefly, and a spark shoots up my arm at her warmth, before she draws hers back. Not a jerk, like she's been stung, but slower, more deliberate, like maybe she doesn't want to. The world seems to tilt for a heartbeat and I grab the first thing I can find.

"Here," I offer, steadying a chair while she wedges it in place. She smiles; this one almost reaches her eyes.

We work in silence for a while, moving trolleys, righting the plant, sliding things back into place. When the last chair is set, she steps back, brushing her palms on her jeans. I catch the faintest tilt of her head, not to me exactly, more like she's telling herself it's enough.

A movement catches my eye. A figure emerges from around the corner, slow, deliberate, head tilting, arms hanging. A zombie, mindlessly wandering.

We exchange a glance, words unnecessary as we retreat further into the mall, ending up at the food court. The food court smells different today. Not bad exactly, just... turning. The glossy apples in the display baskets look dull, skins losing their snap. The bananas have turned freckled, the kind of overripe where you know they won't last, and there's a sweet, cloying note in the air that wasn't there yesterday.

We pass the butcher's counter. The deep freezers are still cool to the touch, but frost is gone from the glass. The meat's fine for now, though you can see it softening at the edges.

"Guess steak's off the menu," I say.

"Oh no, how will I survive without a full slab of cow before noon?"

"Technically, it's afternoon...

She slaps my arm, "Technically, only you can ruin everything fun."

We walk by the bakery stand; a tray of banana-bran

muffins sits under a glass dome. I jump the counter and grab a couple, squeezing a little. They've gone a bit dense, but they'll do.

I slide across the counter, my feet dangling over the edge and tap the space next to me, holding the muffin up as bait.

Hannah crosses her arms over her chest and stares, her eyes flicking from me to the muffin. "You really think I'm going to fall for that?"

Flashing a quick smile, I lean in. "Technically, I'm offering it freely. It's all very generous of me."

"Technically, I can get my own."

"Technically, you have to get past me first."

She huffs, not really annoyed, more amused before jumping on the counter and sidling up beside me. Her shoulder brushes mine, the heat of her skin radiating through my shirt. She snatches the muffin from my hand and takes a bite.

She chews slowly, partly because she ripped a large chunk into her mouth, partly because the muffins are dry and gluggy. When she finally swallows, she turns her head to me. "I should have taken my chances with the steak."

My mouth quirks as I study the way her lips move when she chews and enjoy the feel of her knee against mine.

We sit munching in silence, the hum of the empty mall around us. Every now and then our hands brush, and I catch her glancing at me, quick, but lingering enough that it sends a jolt through me.

Swallowing the last of my breakfast my eyes sweep the deserted food court, catching the abandoned tables, the empty shelves behind the counters.

"What now?" She faces me as she polishes off her last bite.

I shrug, "Afternoon stroll?"

Sliding off the counter, I offer her my arm. She lingers, before jumping off and weaving her arm through mine. Tension ratcheting up my spine, I take a steadying breath and lead the way.

We make our way past darkened storefronts and emergency lights that hum low in the corridors. The empty mall stretching ahead like a playground for the two of us.

We walk past a few shops till I spot the basket of balls at the entrance to the sports shop. It's a natural reaction; I untangle our arms and rush over to the basket, grabbing a ball and bouncing it on my foot then my knee.

She leans against the doorframe, arms crossed, lips twitching. "Careful, Slick, don't hurt yourself."

"Me? I am a well-oiled machine."

"You're definitely something."

Ignoring her jabs, I flick the ball up and catch it behind my back, letting it roll down my other arm.

"Am I meant to be impressed?"

"Impressed, intimidated, whichever works..." I spot a small stack of mats at the back of the store, with a plastic mobile goal.

"You wouldn't be able to intimidate a squirrel with that trick," her head tilts, eyes glinting with challenge.

My mouth curls into a smile. I spin the ball on my finger. "Squirrels fear me. They call me the apex predator of the playground."

She laughs, stepping closer. "Apex predator with Olympic-level footwork? I'll believe it when I see it."

I give the ball a fancy little bounce, tapping it off my knee. "Watch and learn."

She raises an eyebrow with a sly half-smile. "I'm ready to be underwhelmed."

I gesture toward the mats and makeshift goal. "Winner gets bragging rights. Loser... has to fetch the next ball."

Her smile widens, and we clear a small space, the game beginning with light kicks, playful jabs, and brushes of hands and shoulders that linger just a second too long. Eyes lock, teeth flash, and the tension coils tighter with every move.

The way she looks at me when I swipe the ball from her, when I block her shot, it's different now, familiar, a spark of mischief lighting her eyes that sets my nerves alight.

She feints left, I lunge right, and our laughter echoes across the narrow space between racks. I catch her around the waist for a second too long to stop her from cheating, and the heat of her body against mine fills up the hollow cavity behind my ribs. Her breath hitches, sharp and quick, and for a heartbeat we just stay there, too close, too aware, neither willing to step back.

Then she shoves me.

Hard.

Breaking the tension, her laugh spilling like sunlight across the aisles. I stumble back, letting her go, the ball bouncing between us, the air between us is charged.

The ball lands closer to me and I grab it with a swift kick, bouncing it off my foot, teasing her with a crooked grin.

I don't notice her shift until it's too late. She darts left, feints right, and with a flick of her ankle she snatches the ball, and kicks.

It rolls straight into the plastic goal.

She's heaving as she throws her hands up, triumphant. "Goal!" She brings her hands to her mouth curling them into a megaphone. The sound bursts out like static, sharp and crackling, bouncing off the walls of the store. "And the crowd rooooooaaaaarrrrrssss." She blows out the sound again.

I can't help but laugh at her antics. "That's one point, the game's not done yet." I try and regain my composure.

"Of course it is. I win, you lose; suck it!"

Hannah brushes past me, her shoulder nudging mine and I stumble, managing a crooked smile, masking the way my body burns whenever she touches me.

"Suck it?" My voice low, playful. My fingers flex by my side. "You're offering favours to the opponent?"

Her mouth twists in a slow deliberate smile, her eyes flick to mine a moment too long, holding, daring, teasing, the electric pull of it, like every laugh, every brush, every glance is a wire between us sparking hotter than it has all day.

For a heartbeat, neither of us move, just existing in that charged space, the ridiculousness of the game fading, leaving the tension raw and sharp.

"I don't need to offer favours..." She shoves me, laughing, breaking the spell, but the feeling lingers, etched into my skin, the way my chest still aches and my fingers still itch from holding her, even for just a second.

I offer her the game ball. "Your reward."

She grabs it, tucking it under her arm. "I thought my reward was bragging rights."

"And I'm sure you'll use them often, even when unnecessary..."

She flashes a sly smile over her shoulder and leaves the shop. I trail behind, unable to keep my eyes off her ass as she sashays it playfully.

We end up at the bookstore. She wanders off down the fiction aisle, brushing her fingers along the spines, while I drop into the couch near the back.

"You're not picking anything?" her voice drifts between the aisles.

"I'm waiting to see what you bring me."

She returns a few minutes later with two books; one for her—a burly man without a shirt glares at me from the cover. She hands me the other one. *'The Complete Idiot's Guide to Football'*.

My head tilts as I look at her face over the book and she quirks a brow. "It'll come in handy.'

I huff. She giggles as she curls up on the opposite end of the same couch.

She reads her book while I occasionally glimpse over mine, but I know she's not really paying attention. Every now and then, she glances at me over the top of the pages, and every time, I pretend not to notice.

But I do.

And it's driving me insane.

I ache for her in a way that makes every inch of me hurt, but this thing between us is just starting to blossom again. It is still so frail and fragile and if I push too hard, I will destroy it.

17. Day 5

06/11/2025

Everything feels heavier. Slower. The mall is still the same, but the air between us is thick now, charged with something neither of us is saying out loud.

She sits across from me at breakfast, tearing off a piece of protein bar, not looking at me. I study the way her fingers move, the way her lips press together. Memorising the rise and fall of her chest, the way her throat moves when she swallows.

It's stupid.

It's nothing.

But it's everything.

"You're staring," she says without glancing up.

"Maybe I'm just appreciating fine dining," I shoot back, lifting my half-eaten bar.

That earns me the smallest twitch of her mouth, almost a smile. Almost.

She unconsciously tucks an errant hair behind her ear

and shifts in her seat, pretending she didn't like the compliment.

We conclude our meagre breakfast and throw away the wrappers. I don't know if we do it out of habit, keeping our environment clean and hygienic, or if a small part of us is keeping the chaos outside while we live in this pristine, untouched bubble, as if we're preserving something.

"How about a rematch?" she says, chin tilted, eyes glinting.

I grin, leaning back against the table. "Not sure that's a good idea."

"Afraid of losing again?"

"I didn't lose; I was distracted." My eyes sweep the length of her body and her cheeks colour.

"Same thing." She flings her hair behind her shoulder and starts to move away.

I fall into step beside her, ready with another comeback, when she suddenly slows. Her gaze snags on the shape ahead, an old vending machine standing against the wall.

"I used to love these." She points at a bag of cheesy chips I haven't seen in shops for years.

"Probably their only customer, it's why they discontinued them."

"What are you talking about, they're delicious."

"Yes, for people without tastebuds."

"Pfftt, your palate is just spoiled by all the gourmet food you had as a child."

"You mean your terrible baking?"

She stiffens for a split-second. "You were ruined well before I got to your taste buds."

The vending machine hasn't been upgraded yet; it still takes cash. I tap my chest and sides. "Looks like I left my change in my other pants."

"You carry change?" She glares at the black jeans I ended up in after our dress-up dinner.

"It's been known to happen." She shoots me a sceptical look. "Let me assure you though, I do have other ways."

She raises an eyebrow.

I push against the machine, trying to rattle it as I plant my feet, drawing strength through my legs and arms, and heave again. The machine stands firmly against my attempt. Every muscle straining, shoulders burning, veins pressing against my skin.

Nothing.

My ego takes a savage hit as heat rises along the back of my neck. Hannah stands amused with her arms crossed over her chest, shaking her head.

"Amateur." She steps up to the machine, squares her stance, and kicks.

A bag of chips tumbles down with a thud.

She laughs, sharp and bright, throwing her head back. The sound of it sends a jolt of electricity through my bones. I want to hear it again. I want to be the reason she laughs like that.

"Seriously?" I bite down my smile. "You cheat at football and at vending machines?"

"A win's a win," she says, crouching to grab the bag.

I edge closer, reaching for the chips, but she holds them out of reach, grinning. "Nope, these are mine."

"But we are in an apocalypse, we have to share *every-thing*." I swallow hard, letting the full impact of the innuendo land. If she realises, she doesn't show it.

"We really don't."

"How do you expect me to survive then?"

"Who says I want you to survive?"

"Ouch." I clutch at my chest yanking out an invisible arrow. "You *need* me to survive."

"Do I now?"

"Yeah, I bring a lot of value to this apocalypse."

She shifts the chip bag and tucks it behind her back. "Such as?"

"Morale boosting. Quick thinking. Excellent bone structure."

"Oh, you're practically a survival essential."

"Exactly. So give me some chips."

She pushes up on her tiptoes and brings her mouth to my ear, her lips feather against my skin. "You have to earn them."

My breath stalls and I raise an eyebrow, pretending my entire core isn't shaken. "Oh, yeah? And how do I do that?"

She holds my gaze, unwavering. Then, with a slow, deliberate smile, she whispers, "Like this."

And she's gone.

Hannah takes off down the corridor, disappearing around a corner.

For a second, I just stand there, waiting for my world to tilt back on its axis. Then I hear it, a giggle, distant but unmistakable. My lips curl up. Alright then.

I follow the sound, stepping lightly, listening for any hint of movement. Another laugh, this time from behind one of the thick columns near the escalator. I stalk toward it, but the moment I peek around, she's already darting away, slipping between racks of clothing in one of the stores.

"You know I'm going to find you," I call out.

"Maybe." Her voice echoes in the cavernous space. Teasing. Close, but not close enough.

Weaving through the aisles, my pulse quickens, my senses sharpen. Every time I think I've got her, she's already slipping away, nothing but a blur and the sound of her laughter trailing behind her.

I catch sight of her ducking behind a doorway, and this time, I don't hesitate. I move fast, rounding the corner before she has the chance to escape again.

Hannah squeals as I grab her wrist and spin her towards me.

My towering shape looms over her, my entire body heaving with breath. I advance, mirroring her until she's backed against the wall.

We're close.

Too close.

Her breath is shallow, her chest rising and falling in quick little movements. I don't pull away. Neither does she. My lips hover perilously close to hers, the distance between us like a blade edge. My eyes flick to her mouth.

Heat radiates between us, crawling over my skin. Being this close to Hannah makes me feel like I could burst into flames. I know what I should do, but every inch of me rebels against it.

"Guess I win," I say, my voice raw in my throat.

Her eyes trace my jaw as it tenses. "Guess you do." Her words are little more than a whisper.

"Where's my prize?"

She lifts the bag of chips, a weak little offering, and for a heartbeat my gaze flicks to it before locking back on her mouth, our bodies an impulse apart. In that moment I can no longer hold back.

I lean in and our lips crash together. A desperate, hungry sound climbs low in my throat, and then my arms are around her, dragging her closer, her breath mixing with mine. My fingers skim up her back, tracing the lines of her body.

She's pinned between me and the wall, her warmth searing through my clothes, her body pressed against mine. I kiss her harder, my grip tightening as I pull her closer. Groaning into her mouth, I swallow the rush of heat that surges through me like wildfire.

Her lips are soft, urgent, completely consuming. Gripping her hair, I tilt her head back to deepen the kiss, to take everything she's offering and more. We're a live wire sparking in all directions, electricity flying unchecked between us. My wild, desolate heart hammers against my ribs. Greedy. Desperate.

I need more.

I want more.

And just then, just when I think I finally have her, when I finally have everything I want, Hannah pushes against my chest, hard, breaking our kiss and forcing me to take a step back, putting unnecessary space between us.

Her head falls back against the wall, as she sucks in ragged breaths, eyes dark with something raw, something I know I put there. She shakes her head slowly, and all I can do is watch, aching for the life we could've had.

"We can't do this."

"Why not? There's obviously something here between us, still. After all this time. I never stopped loving you."

"But you loved your money more."

The sting thrums through my body. "Hannah." I try to close the distance between us again, but she spins away from the wall, no longer the pliable, yielding Hannah that was just curled around me. "I was a stupid kid, I told my mum what she wanted to hear and then I looked for you. For six weeks I ran around that town searching. You vanished. I picked you, not the money. I would have married you. You were the one who pushed me away."

"You would have kept me a secret."

"No, I wouldn't have." Frustration builds inside me, our last conversation flooding my senses.

"Your mum was right. You needed better."

"No, I only ever needed you. There was never anyone better."

"You have proved the contrary."

"No." I step closer to her but she steps back. "Not one of those women were better." I take another step as she retreats again. "Not a single one of them meant anything." For every step she takes back, I match her stride forward, closing the space until her legs hit the couch "Not a single one of them were you, Hannah."

"It doesn't change things." She rolls away from the couch as I reach out for her waist. "You discarded me."

"I didn't know what was important then. You can't punish me forever for being a stupid kid."

"Stupid rich kid."

"Yes," I sigh. "Stupid rich kid."

"Entitled, spoiled—"

"Yes."

"Obnoxious."

"Sure."

"With terrible dress sense."

"Hey—" I protest, frowning. "That's just uncalled for. I've always been stylish."

A ghost of a smile toucher her lips before slipping away.

I move towards her again. "I'm sorry."

She's backed herself against another wall and her eyes sweep the room searching for an escape. "It's too late," she growls at me but it's weak.

"It's not too late, we have another chance. You said you'd love me till the world ended."

"I didn't say I'd love you after." She shrugs and tries to walk past me, but this time I grab her arm and push her back against the wall.

"You're lying." I search her eyes.

"No, that's what you're good at." With that she wrenches herself free and leaves.

Hannah walks away, and I let her go.

Again.

I rake a hand through my hair, gripping the strands at the back of my head as I watch her disappear around the corner. My pulse drums against my throat, the echo of her touch still searing my body.

I draw in a long breath and stare at the empty space she's left behind. I can't accept what she said, I won't. There was urgency in her kiss, heat in her touch—and, more than anything, the way she looked at me, like maybe, just maybe, she was finally letting me in again.

This push and pull is wearing me down. Every time we're on the brink of something real, she slams the door, leaving me outside in the cold.

I'm running out of time.

※※※※※

Her name echoes off the hollow walls of the mall, swallowed by emptiness.

"Hannah?" My voice cracks on the second syllable. No answer. Just the humming silence that seems to linger here, broken only by the faint creak of metal somewhere far away.

I keep searching.

Step after step, the ache in my chest grows heavier. We are no longer playing, and this time there is so much more at stake. I drag myself past storefronts, the mannequins frozen in their cheerful poses, mocking me with their plastic smiles, bright and unfeeling in the dim glow of the emergency lights.

The bookstore comes first—where we sat on the couch just last night, trading pages back and forth like it meant something. My fingertips slide over the spines, peering between aisles, calling her name, but nothing answers. No Hannah.

I move on. Sporting goods. The café. The food court. Each corner I turn, I hear her laugh for half a second in my head, the way it rang out earlier, my pulse knocking at my throat at the imaginary sound. I chase it, desperate, only to find the echo was my own mind playing tricks.

The guilt comes in waves.

Every shadow I pass hauls me back to the playground, to the way she looked at me after hearing my mother's voice, dripping with disdain. I should've defended her. I should've chosen her without hesitation. Instead, I let cowardice win. I told her she'd have to be a secret, like something shameful I couldn't claim. Her face, broken, and shattered—unrecognisable. And as much as I wanted to blame it on my mother, it was all my doing. And then she was gone.

Six weeks.

Six weeks of searching.

Six weeks of her absence like a hollow in my chest, each day another reminder that I'd destroyed something I couldn't live without. I looked everywhere, every park, every street, every shop, every street and friends' homes I had access to, but she was gone. And I carried that emptiness all the way to college, and it never left. It's still here now, gnawing at me.

"Hannah!" My voice rips through the deserted clothing store. The racks stand untouched, clothes limp, lifeless. My words bounce back, brittle and thin. I clench my fists until my knuckles burn. Another step. Another disappointment. Every empty aisle is another knife, another cut that doesn't stop bleeding.

Hours pass like this. The sun sinks, leaving the mall colder, its corridors sinking into shadow. I've scoured every level, every shop. My throat is raw from calling her name. My legs ache. And still nothing. Just silence, just ghosts.

By the time I make it back to the camping store, I'm hollowed out. Defeated. My chest an empty cavity where hope used to live. I push the door open and step inside, the quiet pressing down heavily, like the mall itself is telling me to give up.

And then I see her.

She's curled on the mattress, her back to me, her face turned toward the wall. Her shoulders rise and fall with the rhythm of her breaths. My throat tightens, my whole body seizing with the relief and the ache of it. She's here. She didn't leave. Not this time. But then again, she couldn't, even if she wanted to.

I stand rooted in place, not daring to move closer, afraid she'll vanish if I do. My voice a rough whisper. "Hannah..."

She doesn't stir. Doesn't answer. She remains silent, as if her world doesn't need me in it.

I lower myself onto the mattress beside her, leaving a space between us, staring up at the ceiling. The dark canvas above feels endless, oppressive. I whisper her name again, fainter this time, but there's still nothing.

We lie there inches apart and yet the distance between us feels endless. I listen to the sound of her steady breathing, letting exhaustion take over. I stare at the ceiling above, cold and empty, a mirror of the ache still clawing inside me, until sleep drags me down.

18. The Midnight Riser
2008

Ethan

This is my favourite time of day; the part when all my chores are done, all the private tutors have gone, when mother allows me an ounce of freedom which I use and abuse by escaping through my bedroom window and biking like a madman to the tiny strip of shops that make up the main street. The strip of shops where Fiona Adler has the most popular bakery in town. And where Hannah works for pocket money after school.

I always make it at closing time, when the bakery has emptied for the day and all that's left is the lingering smell of pastry and people. Ghosts of perfume and fondant. I sneak in through the back door that Fiona pretends she doesn't leave open for me and crouch behind the counter, heart hammering like I'm robbing the place.

Fiona is finishing up, going through her usual routine, counting up her earnings for the day.

Hannah moves around the kitchen like she owns it, her hair in a bun, humming some old indie song under her breath. She hangs her apron on the back wall to reveal flour on her jeans and the oversized hoodie I left here a week ago. My breath hitches at the sight of it drowning her frame, sleeves pushed up, like she's taken a part of me and tangled herself inside it.

Fiona's voice calls from the front. "Hannah?"

Hannah skates by me and gives me a quick smile as she pokes her head around the corner to Fiona. "Yeah?"

"We seem to have a little extra money in the till today."

Hannah shrugs. "I have no idea where it came from." Her cheeks colour and she shifts. Hannah is a terrible liar.

"Think it has something to do with the rat problem we've been having?"

"The rat problem?" Hannah's voice breaks a little and she looks over her shoulder.

"Yeah, the giant one that shows up here every night you work and eats half the leftovers."

"I... Um..."

"Just tell him his money is no good here, as long as he makes you happy."

"I. Um..."

"That boy does make you happy, doesn't he?"

Hannah looks down for a second like she has been busted, and guilt settles over her. But when she looks up it's at me, her smile genuine and affectionate, and it takes every part of me to remain hidden and not rush to her, take her in my arms and kiss her. "He really, really does."

"Mmm hmm, good, but—"

"But?" She swallows hard.

"If he ruins another lemon tart, I swear to all the gods I'm putting his face on a banned poster and locking that back door twenty minutes early!"

Hannah covers her giggle by clearing her throat. "Yeah

okay, I'll pass the message on to any rats I see running around."

"Good, and to any currently hiding behind the kitchen counter would also be great."

The pink on Hannah's cheeks intensifies and she grins, tilting her head, mischief flickering in her eyes. All I can do is picture Fiona folding her arms across her large frame and pretending to be stern. That woman doesn't have a single hard edge.

"Okay, darling, I'm off. Don't forget to lock the back door."

"I won't," Hannah replies sweetly, wiping her hands on a tea towel and shooting me a look.

We wait, listening for her footsteps to fade down the alley.

Then the silence swells.

We're alone.

"Think she knows about us?" I whisper.

Hannah flicks her tea towel at me. "No, I think we are totally pulling it off."

"You think?"

"Of course, not like you sneak in like a raccoon in heat or anything."

"Can't help it, you make me hot."

"You are going to make me unemployed."

"That will never happen, Fiona clearly approves."

"Barely tolerates," Hannah corrects, but there's a smile in her voice.

I cross the room in three strides and catch her by the waist before she can dodge me. She lets out a squeak, muffled when I kiss her temple, cheek, jaw. She smells like sugar and warm dough and something sharp beneath it, like citrus, or secrets.

"You have flour in your eyebrow," I murmur.

"You have icing on your neck."

"Want to lick it off?"

She shoves me lightly. "You're disgusting."

"You're obsessed."

"You wish."

I do. I wish constantly. Obsessively. Every damn night.

I take her in. Those beautiful brown eyes, the flour flakes hanging on to her eyebrow, her shining wet lips and that messy bun that I want so desperately to unravel. This woman reduces me to a series of compulsions, and I give in because tonight I am tired. I'm tired of holding back, I'm tired of sneaking in and I'm tired of always waiting.

A lightning strike sensation travels along my body as I find her mouth with mine and kiss her like I'm trying to memorise the shape of her lips. A sudden noise has us both jumping and we break apart. Car tyres on gravel. We flinch, drop to the floor like fugitives. We laugh out our relief once we realise it's just someone leaving the parking lot.

"Well, that was close," I say, trying to catch my breath, keeping the humour rolling. "Saved your life there. You owe me one."

Hannah's eyes narrow, but she's grinning. "Saved my life? From what? A car backing out of its parking spot?"

"Yes!"

"But we are inside!"

"You have a strange way of saying thank you."

"Thank you?"

"You're welcome!"

"What? No!"

"No? Are you denying that I am your hero?"

"Hero? You landed on a whisk."

"It was a tactical sacrifice. For the record, I'd land on a whole baking tray if it meant saving your life again."

"You used to have standards."

"I lost those the minute you fed me burnt croissants and told me it was an 'artistic choice.'"

She leans in slightly, an evil little grin curving her lips. "You keep coming back though."

"Someone has to keep rescuing you."

"From your terrible humour?"

"Shh. You're ruining the mood."

"What mood?"

"My good mood. Or the great mood I'll be in after you thank me."

"You're still on that?"

"Yes, I deserve thanks, my bravery deserves to be acknowledged."

She lets out a theatrical breath, edging closer, her face inches from mine. "I could," she says.

"You should." I swallow hard.

"Oh?" She leans closer still and sweeps her tongue over her lower lip. "Not sure I could put it into words."

"Yeah?" My voice comes out lower than I expect.

She meets my eyes, heat rushing into her cheeks, and mine too, because suddenly the air feels thinner, tighter. I lean in and kiss that soft place where her neck meets her shoulder, and her whole body shivers beneath my hands.

"I think it's something I need to show you."

It's muffled against my hair, her lips a hairsbreadth away from my ear, but I know what I heard. The entire world stands still for a tiny but certain eternity; the air is vacuumed from my lungs and my vision blurs. My pulse battering with the weight of her answer.

I pretend that I am completely fine, pulling back just enough so that our eyes lock. "Show me?"

"Show you," she whispers, taking the lead. Her mouth captures mine in a staggering kiss that has me questioning everything. Her hands weave through my hair and her body is suddenly so close there is no air between us.

I pull away, breathless. "You sure?" My jaw tightens, nerves twitching beneath my skin.

"I'm sure." Her eyes find mine, tender and creased with anxious nervousness that I am sure mirrors my own.

I don't wait for Hannah to change her mind. It's selfish, but I am starving for her, and after all, I am her hero and she is my reward.

I kiss her, slow and lingering, pouring every ounce of how much I love her, want her, *need* her into the space between us. Her hands find the hem of my shirt and tug it up. I let it fall to the floor without a second thought.

She drags her long fingers down my back leaving heated trails along my skin. My entire world is focused solely on one thing. Hannah.

We break apart and I smooth my discarded shirt over the floor, a makeshift sheet, before she leans back to lie on it. Her gaze sweeps my torso, my face, my hands. The way she looks at me, like I'm enough, *more* than enough, makes my pulse race.

I settle above her, muscles taut, heart pounding. We're both new at this. We fumble a little, laugh a little, nerves tangled with adrenaline, but it's beautiful. Real. Every part of it.

I press my forehead to hers as the world holds its breath. Looking into Hannah's eyes this close feels like staring at a sunrise, too bright, too much, and absolutely impossible to look away from. For a short while, I leave my body and become a part of her, and all I know is that I wish I could put all my feelings in a bottle and capture them forever.

For the first time in my short life, I understand what it means to belong to someone completely. "I love you," I whisper, my voice guttural and breathy.

She shivers beneath me, and whispers it back, "I love you too."

I kiss her again, losing myself, all my defences give way.

When we pull apart, she looks around the room till she finds her shirt and pulls it over herself, suddenly feeling exposed, vulnerable. I release a slow breath and reluctantly slip into my boxers, leaving my shirt under her still-naked, beautiful ass. And lie down again beside her.

I take her in, this new Hannah. Flushed, sweaty, red-faced and broad smile. This girl that transformed into a woman beneath me, who has turned me into a man. I want so badly to take her hand in mine, to walk down the street of Valenwood and announce that she's mine and I'm hers. But despite being the worst kept secret in town, we still sneak around, because my parents don't know yet, and Hannah's parents definitely wouldn't approve.

But here, with the world shut out by a locked front door and a humming refrigerator, we get to be just us.

"I don't want to do this anymore."

She stiffens.

"I mean," I rush to add, "I don't want us to be a secret anymore. I'm tired of the sneaking and the hiding, it's exciting and all, but... "

"It's exhausting," she finishes.

My throat tightens around the words. "Imagine what we could be doing with our time if we weren't hiding behind cookie displays."

She shoots me a playful look. "I mean, didn't look like

you hated what we just did hiding behind this cookie display..."

I grab her and inhale her scent. "Don't get me wrong. That was ... the fucking most amazing thing in my whole life, but this is definitely not the place I wanted our first time to be... you deserve better."

Her face stains with red and she gives me a shy smile. My body feels like lava, hot and melting and ready to burn her all over again.

"This," she waves her hands over the space, "it's not forever."

"No?"

"Just until we finish school. Just until the year ends. Then maybe—"

"Maybe what?"

"Maybe we tell people. Maybe we stop sneaking. Maybe we walk through the front door instead of the back."

I reach for her hand. She lets me hold it. "You know I'd wait forever, right?" I whisper.

"Don't say that."

"Why not?"

"Because I might actually start to believe you."

"You should. I've been in love with you since you made me eat your ruined lemon tart and told me it was supposed to taste like sadness."

Her laugh is quiet but bright. "It did."

"It did. But I ate every bite."

"Idiot."

"Only for you."

There's a long pause, filled with the quiet hum of bakery silence and the sound of our breathing syncing. Then she turns, legs tucked up and kisses me.

It's not quick. It's not timid. It's the kind of kiss that

speaks in full sentences. The kind that says, *I miss you. I need you. I can't believe we just did that.*

When we finally break apart, her forehead presses to mine.

There's so much I want to tell her, so much more I want to do, explore, enjoy. A lifetime of wants sits cross-legged on bakery tiles, covered in flour and she's looking at me like she wants the same.

"Fiona is going to kill us," she whispers.

"Way to kill the mood."

She giggles and plucks one of my few chest hairs.

"Ow!" She giggles again and the sound burns me. "She doesn't have to know." I grab her hand, pulling it away as she tries to attack another defenceless hair.

"That woman finds out everything."

Hannah wants to pull away and get ready to leave but I am not ready yet, not ready to relinquish her warmth, the way her limbs are tangled with mine, the way she smells and tastes.

"I have to get home."

I tilt my head once, a quiet defeat, reluctant to let this evening end. My legs feel like jelly as I try to stand, try to walk Hannah to the door, try not to reach for her again. But I do. I always do.

She shrugs on her coat, eyes flicking up to mine, that familiar sadness pressing gently against the corners of her smile. Like leaving me hurts just a little—and God, that makes it worse. Makes it better too.

At the back door, I loop my arms around her waist, pulling her into one last hug. She melts into it like she always does, forehead against my chest, her breath warm through my shirt. I want to ask her to stay. Just five more minutes. Just until the stars disappear. But I don't. Because she can't.

"I wish we didn't have to do this," she murmurs.

"Me too," I whisper into her hair. "But I don't regret doing any of it."

She pulls back just enough to kiss me, a deep bruising kiss, like she's memorising the shape of my mouth. Like it has to last her until the next time.

I open the door for her, and she steps into the night.

"I'll message when I'm home," she says.

"Use the code name, The Midnight Riser," I tease, trying to lighten the weight sitting heavy in my chest.

"The Midnight Riser?"

"My new superhero name."

"And how did you come up with that?"

"Well, we're in a bakery and we just…"

She shoves me hard, her laugh trills. "Stop."

"But you make it so *hard*." I make sure she has no illusions about the innuendo.

"Ethan," she whines, letting out a short, breathless laugh.

"Difficult," I say, pulling her into yet another kiss. "So fucking difficult," I whisper and release her, pushing her body away from mine, forcing the distance.

Hannah casts one last glance over her shoulder. And then she's gone.

The door clicks shut.

I lean against it, eyes closed, holding onto the ghost of her scent and the warmth still lingering on my skin.

Another night over. Another secret kept. Another piece of her tucked deeper into the space she's carved inside me.

And tomorrow, I'll want her just the same, and I'd hide behind every counter in this town, if it meant I got to love her again.

19. Dinner with the Greenes

07/10/2025

The Greenes are more artificial than the vanilla spray scenting my mother's sitting room. Mrs Greene is more plastic than human, her silicon tits are way too big for her petite frame, and she's draped in a shiny dress that's adorned in glittering jewels. Her husband is stuffed into a too-small tux that looks brand new; they look ridiculous, like pigeons trying to be peacocks.

Miranda—known to all her friends as Sookie—on the other hand, is dressed in a modest black dress that looks like it's been bought at some trendy flea market. The thin straps expose her heavily tattooed arms and shoulders and her ears are bowed low with heavy hooped earrings.

Our parents exchange the usual greetings, kissing each other's cheeks without actually showing any affection, as Martha hands them each a flute of Champagne which they drain in savage gulps.

I stare at the door, mapping my nearest exit.

"Searching for an escape route?" Sookie comes to stand by me and we glance at the door together.

"You know it."

She leans in to kiss my cheek, and I give her an affectionate hug. "How are you, babe?" she asks me, her eyes glinting with a dose of mischief.

"Living the dream." I look dreamily into the distance.

"Like the one with Freddy Kruger in it?"

"Exactly like that, but with all the screaming and none of the killing."

"Dramatic much?"

"I try." I shrug and her mouth splits in a knowing grin.

Sookie pulls out a cigarette and puts it to her mouth, beckoning me to follow her to the balcony. I easily oblige.

"So, I hear we are getting set up," I say as Sookie brings her silver Zippo to the tip of the cigarette, the amber setting her face a shade of orange as she inhales deeply.

"So I hear." Her words come out in a gush of grey smoke.

"What does Angie think about it?"

"She thinks it's hilarious."

"That's because she doesn't have to sit through dinner with my mother." I purse my lips.

"But I do, and I made her promise that when I get home she better make it *all better*." She bites her bottom lip and runs a hand along the curve of her body. My cock jolts in my pants. It's not because I want Sookie in any way, but I am a fucking man. The idea of another woman kissing her or doing anything for that matter.... I take a safe step back. She notices and her laugh sparks like static in the narrow space. "What about you, cowboy?"

"No one's called me that since New York."

"That's cause no one here knows about New York."

"And we're going to keep it that way." My eyebrow hooks up, daring her to contradict me.

"We'll see."

"Will we now?" I close the distance between us, and she lets out a shriek as I dig into the sensitive flesh just above her hips, that ticklish spot I discovered on an overindulgent night out and never let her forget I remembered.

She shrieks, the smoke falling from her mouth in a broken waterfall. "Okay, okay, no one will find out," she gasps between choked giggles, and I relent.

My mother chooses that moment to walk on to the balcony. Her gaze sweeps over us; the close proximity, my hand just above her hip, the delighted smile still on Sookie's face. "Good, you're getting acquainted." Her tone is the same as always; dour and cool, but I did notice the flicker of delight in her eye. "Dinner is in five minutes."

We share a brief glance and Mother leaves.

I back away from Sookie letting her smoke what's left of her cigarette. "She didn't send her spy."

"Obviously didn't trust them to deliver an accurate report."

She tips her head slightly, a crooked grin tugging at her mouth. "She's not exactly walking away with an accurate report either."

"Who cares, she'll believe what she wants anyway."

"Yup." She takes a final drag before killing the butt in the ashtray. "You didn't answer my question."

"Oh, would you look at that? It's dinner time." I hook my arm through hers and lead us inside before she asks anything else.

Sookie gives me a sideways glance but stays quiet. She's always been good like that, great for a laugh, a party and a few helpers to really get things wild, but also tactical and understanding. I know she will let things go, but only for now...

†††††

Dinner with the Greenes could have been lovely; but my mother, as always, makes it an arduous affair. The over-the-top compliments, exaggerated laughter, and unnecessary comments about my future with their daughter. All the 'adults' in the room make dismissive comments about Sookie's 'little roommate'. It has her stiff and agitated by my side as they continue talking about us like we're pieces on a chessboard placed perfectly for a checkmate.

Sookie's father eyes me like I'm the goose that laid the golden eggs, except that he wants me to lay his daughter instead and pass the gold over to him. "Strapping young lad you've grown into. Your father must be proud."

"Wouldn't know, he's too busy being dead."

Sookie almost chokes on her drink and my mother gives me a stern look.

"Oh, well... you know what I meant of course," Mr. Greene stammers, trying to keep his tone light.

"Of course," I don't look up as I cut into my steak.

"Such a shame. Going so young."

"Yes, we're all devastated," Not bothering to tame the bitterness in my voice, "aren't we, Mother?"

She lifts her glass, sipping slow. I know this move, she's settling her anger, letting the tiny drop of alcohol soothe her savage tongue before something slips out, and thinking about a response that would be socially acceptable.

"We are indeed," she sets her glass down, "and such a shame he won't be around to see you marry."

"Our children do look good together," Mr Greene smiles at us across the table.

Sookie rolls her eyes, her shoulders stiff. "What about Angie?"

"Your little roommate? I'm sure she can find other accommodation, you've mentioned she is employed." Mrs. Greene waves a hand dismissively, as if the very thought of Angie is a phase Sookie should have outgrown by now.

"Angie isn't my '*roommate*'," Sookie intonates the words as she says them. "She's my girlfriend."

Mr. Greene makes a vague hand motion, as if to wave her words aside, then turns to his plate and slices into his steak. "Yes, darling, we know you are close to her and as we've said before, it's good for young women to have close friendships, but eventually, you'll have to settle down properly. Find a nice man."

"I don't need or want a man," Sookie's nose flares, "when Angie eats my pussy just fine."

A deathly silence falls across the table as I cough to hide my laugh and shift to hide my hard-on. Sookie stands up. "Excuse me, I'm going for a smoke."

"We're in the middle of dinner," her mother, whose cheeks are redder than the wine, admonishes her.

"It's okay, let her go, you know how restless kids are." My mother's voice is all poison.

Sookie doesn't seem to care; she's already halfway out the door.

"I'll go check..." I'm out of my seat and following without further fanfare, behind me cutlery cuts through the heavy silence.

I find her leaning on the balcony, smoke curling from her mouth. "You okay?" It's a stupid question but an easy opener.

"Yeah, no, it doesn't matter."

"Of course it does."

She inhales sharply, smoke trembling between her fingers. "I wish they'd stop living in fucking denial and just accept that Angie is a permanent part of my life." She shakes her head, jaw tight. "It's frustrating. I have to deal with bullshit from everyone else, but I thought, at the very least, my own family would get it."

"Well, they definitely get that she eats your pussy."

Sookie's hoarse raspy laugh unspools some of the tightness from her features. "Family. Can't live with 'em, can't kill 'em."

"Kill them with kindness?"

"That would take too long."

I scratch my chin, pulling my mouth down as if I am in deep thought. "Alternatively, give it time; work stress and too much fatty food works like magic... just ask my dad."

She chokes on her gasp and lets out a barking laugh. "Dark."

"Could be darker."

"I know." A faint curve touches her mouth, and the strain in her expression fades. "Doesn't matter, though. Angie and I, we built something real. She's my family now. And honestly? That's enough."

"Careful now, if you keep talking that way I might start believing there is a soul behind that darkness."

"Says *Pitch Black* over here." Sookie's mouth cracks in another smile as smoke cascades from between her thick red lips. After a beat, she tilts her head toward me. "What about you? Anyone in the picture?"

"We're back to that are we?"

She shrugs and drags.

A crooked grin tugging at my mouth. "No one."

Her brow lifts. "Really?"

I hesitate. "Ran into Hannah the other day."

Sookie blinks, surprised. "Wait. Hannah? *The* Hannah?"

I lift a shoulder in quiet confirmation.

She whistles low. "Damn. So what are you gonna do about it?"

"Nothing."

"Nothing?"

"Yeah, nothing. She won't talk to me, won't acknowledge my existence, won't even look at me except for that one time she had me arrested."

"So?"

"So? I've tried."

"Clearly not hard enough."

"Trust me, I've tried."

She keeps staring at me, unimpressed. Then, after a beat, she shifts, turning to fully face me. "First, we will circle back to your arrest, but babe… if the world was ending tomorrow, what would you do?"

I frown. "What?"

"If you knew, without a doubt, that you had less than twenty-four hours left. No consequences, no future to plan for, nothing holding you back. Would you still do nothing, would you still try to convince me that you've tried everything?" She tilts her head. "Or would you find her, would you fight harder?"

I let the silence fill the space I can't, my gaze slides to my mother's manicured rose garden below.

She doesn't let up. "Maybe the reason we don't love unreasonably is because we think we have time. We make excuses, we hesitate because we believe there's always later. But what if there isn't?"

I swallow, my grip tightening on the railing. Me and Hannah always said we'd love each other till the world ends. But Hannah stopped loving me long before it did.

Sookie steps closer, voice softer now. "What if it all ends tomorrow?"

I drag a hand through my hair, letting out a slow breath. "But it won't."

She shrugs. "Maybe. Maybe not. But what if it does?"

Silence stretches between us.

Sookie fills it with a sharp inhale.

A thin ribbon of smoke drifts upward as she leans closer, "How much do you love her?"

I stare past her, my jaw tight, my throat working against the weight of the words I don't want to say. She waits, patient, giving me space to either answer or let the silence swallow the moment whole.

"I can't quantify what I feel for Hannah. It's the kind of love that ruins you. The kind that gets under your skin, into your blood. You can leave, you can try to move on, but it never really lets you go. It follows you, haunts you. It shapes the way you breathe, the way you think, the way you see the world. And no matter how much distance, how much time, there's always that pull, like a thread wrapped around your ribs, leading right back to them."

I shake my head; a humourless laugh drifts between us.

"So yeah, that's how much."

I finally meet Sookie's gaze. There's something unreadable in her eyes, a flicker of understanding, or maybe pity. I choose not to question it.

"That feels like a lot."

I tilt my head back for a moment, eyes closed, then let it fall forward.

"Yeah," I admit. "Sometimes it feels like too much. But then it might all be false, an echo of everything I felt before, all the emotions of a young, confused boy who had his heart broken. I put Hannah on a pedestal, and no one ever came close."

"So, you've never felt that way about anyone else?"

"Nope."

"And when you saw her the other day after all that time, how did you feel?"

"Like I'd do *anything* to have her back just so I can stop yearning for something that should have always been mine. I want Hannah, I always have. I'm deeply, pathetically and endlessly in love with that woman."

"Or completely obsessed."

"Maybe love and obsession are the same thing. Like I said, there are times I feel like I'm chasing a shadow—a mere idea of a childhood crush, but then no one has ever challenged me, infuriated me, annoyed me and disrespected me like Hannah has."

"Mommy issues much?"

I nudge Sookie with my shoulder, but she's unphased. "No, it's not like that, she's the only one who has ever been honest with me. She's not afraid of my money or my family, she calls me on my shit, she doesn't dance around the issues. She sets everything inside me on fire."

Sookie studies me for a long moment, then nods once, satisfied. She leans back against the railing, her expression thoughtful.

"So, then do whatever it takes."

"She's made it clear that she will not speak to me unless I'm the last person left on earth, and even then, it is questionable."

"What exactly did she say?"

"That she won't speak to me *even* if I was the last man on earth."

Sookie's cigarette glows as she draws in a long, deliberate breath before letting the smoke drift between us. She punches the butt of her cigarette on the ashtray, a cloud of smoke curling from her mouth.

"Well then, you should probably figure out how to become the last person on earth."

"But —" An idea strikes me, sharp, brilliant, totally crazy, unfolding like lightning across my mind. I clear my throat. "You still working for that studio? The special effects thing?"

She huffs out a laugh, like she can't believe I'd change the subject, but she lets me. "Yeah. Why?"

My eyes sweep over the town as the idea takes shape inside my mind. "I might need some help."

20. Day 6

0/11/2025

Pacing the £3 store, I curse at the universe as the satellite phone powers up. I stare at the blue screen, reading over the waiting message.

'*How is it going in there?*'

I start typing my frustration. '*I was so close. We kissed. And then she backed away again.*'

I watch the screen. Three dots blink, then vanish. Then blink again.

'*Maybe you're a terrible kisser.*'

'*Wow, thanks. Super useful.*'

The dots blink again. My jaw tightens. '*How much longer are you gonna be?*'

I sigh and pinch the bridge of my nose. "As long as I need," I mutter.

'*Look, I'm close. She wants it. I know she does. She just doesn't trust it yet.*'

The reply comes fast this time.

'Okay. Just know things are beginning to unravel here. We can't hold much longer.'

That cold knot in my stomach tightens. I stare at the words until the screen dims.

'Just keep it together. I only need a little more time. I'm close. I can feel it. She just needs a little nudge. I'll figure it out.'

'Leave the nudge to me, I've got you.'

'What does that mean?'

There are no more dots, no more replies. I tilt my head back and blow out a breath toward the ceiling then stash the phone in its hiding place, burying my secrets with it.

My pulse thuds in my ears. I make my way to the food court and lean against a kiosk counter, rubbing my hand over my face and wondering what the hell is going on out there. The silence is thick, like the whole mall is holding its breath.

And then, everything goes black.

The emergency lights don't flicker. They *snap*. Gone in an instant. The backup hum of the emergency power dies with them. Dead silence. Darkness swallows the space like a vacuum.

"Hannah?" My voice cuts through it, sharp and sudden. I push off the counter, heartbeat spiking. "Hannah!"

A sound rises out of the dark.

A thump.

A screech.

A furious, low roar.

Then all at once:

Bang. Bang. Bang.

The windows.

They're slamming into the glass like a tidal wave,

snarling and shrieking, fists and bodies thudding against the doors. The sound is deafening, like the mall itself is groaning under pressure.

"Hannah!" I shout, trying to be heard over the noise, stumbling forward into the pitch blackness, tripping over chairs and running into tables. I can't see a damn thing.

"Ethan!" Her voice snaps through, panicked, distant.

I race toward the sound, nearly slipping on the slick floor, heart clawing up my throat. Shapes move in the dark, my brain tells me they're shadows, but my coursing adrenaline says otherwise. I don't stop. She could be hurt, cornered, alone. I need to get to her.

"Keep talking!" I yell.

"I'm here—by the fountain!" Her answer comes thin and strained.

I find her in the dark, fingers gripping my arm the second I'm close enough. She clutches on to me as if I am her only lifeline, her hot breath rushing against my body as she tucks herself into me.

"Come on," I say, grabbing her hand. "Camping store. Now."

We creep against the walls feeling our way along them making our way to the only place we feel safe.

We're flying blind, feet pounding across tile, carpet and cracked linoleum, the screech of the undead at the windows swelling behind us. It's primal. Terrifying. Like the whole place might cave in any second.

We reach the store, and snake through the aisles to the safety of the office, our makeshift weapons and cosy tent over the bed where the illusion of safety awaits.

My hands shake as I throw the door open, shove her inside, and slam it shut, cutting off the worst of the noise, though the muffled pounding, glass shuddering, and metal creaking still seep through.

It's even darker inside, the thick door blocking the chaos outside but not erasing it. I fumble around the table, hands dragging along the smooth surface till I find one of the LED lanterns and switch it on. A warm yellow light spills out, soft and flickering.

Hannah flinches against it at first, like the light's too sudden after all that black, but she adjusts quickly and blinks up at me.

Her cheeks are flushed, her hair tangled and falling in her face, breath tearing and out of her, eyes wild. And I can't help but think that she's the most beautiful thing I've ever seen.

"You hurt?" My voice scrapes out rough. Too rough.

She shakes her head too fast. "No. You?"

"No." but her eyes scan me like she's checking for injuries or maybe like she doesn't believe I'm real. Like maybe she almost lost me and doesn't know what to do with the fact that I'm standing right here.

"I didn't know where you were," she grips her arms, nails digging into her flesh. "You didn't answer. I thought—" She breaks off, jaw clenched like she's trying to bite the words back. "I thought you were out there. That they got you."

"I was concentrating on hearing you above all the noise." I shake my head. "They were pounding so loud I could barely hear your voice."

She steps forward. Not all the way, but close. Close enough that it vibrates under my skin.

"I thought you were gone," her voice drops to a whisper. "I thought I was too late."

"You weren't." I close the space between us. "I'm right here."

She reaches for me, clutching the front of my hoodie and pressing her forehead to my chest like she's trying to ground herself, like I'm the only solid thing left in a world that's spinning too fast.

I hold her. Carefully. One arm around her back, one hand curled around the back of her head. The pounding outside keeps going, but it feels distant now, muted by the rhythm of our breathing.

"I don't want to lose you," she says.

"You won't."

"I mean it, Ethan."

"I know." I rest my hand on the back of her neck, holding her there. "Me too."

Then she looks up, eyes burning.

And I don't move.

I wait.

Her grip tightens in the fabric of my hoodie.

She drags herself upward, eyes locked on mine.

Her mouth slams into mine.

She's raw and urgent, electric, crashing into me like I'm the only thing keeping her upright. She kisses me with every shred of adrenaline still rushing through her, and I kiss her back like it might be the last time I ever get to.

Hannah pushes against me, ripping the air from my lungs, wrapping herself around my hardening body. My hands fold around her back, and I draw her closer, kissing her harder, before she can draw air, before she can come to her senses. My need all encompassing.

I lift Hannah by her ass and she wraps her legs around me. My body aches for her—years of unanswered desire raging in my veins as I fight to control my actions, my reactions.

I walk us towards the wall, where I pin her body, cup the back of her neck, and tip her head back, deepening our kiss. Since our kiss yesterday, I haven't stopped thinking about her sweet mouth, about kissing her again, tasting her, and I don't know how I am ever going to stop. I drag my mouth away, letting her catch her breath, fearing that with every inhale, she'll come to her senses.

Hannah devours me with her eyes, threading her hand through my hair, as if she can't quite believe I'm not part of an illusion. My gaze searches her face, part of me still waiting for her to change her mind.

"Hannah," I breathe her name as I trail kisses along her neck. "Are you sure?"

And just like that I am transported to a world far away, to a night that feels like a lifetime away, when the most beautiful girl in the world let me have her on a bakery floor. I am instantly harder and intensely terrified.

She places a hand over my chest, to my heart. I am completely aware of how wildly it pounds for her, *because* of her. I guess part of me believes that she's seeking comfort in my body because she's terror stricken by her ordeal. Up until that moment, it hadn't occurred to me that she might truly want me too.

"Yes," she whispers back and finds my mouth, erasing all my doubts. All the tenderness vanishes, my hands roaming everywhere, exploring her.

Her body is both foreign territory and a familiar land. She is no longer a teenager on the verge of womanhood. Her large breasts fill my palms as I squeeze and pull, her ass is full and I grasp the flesh wanting more of her, all of her, all at once. I rip her shirt off her body, letting it vanish in the darkness.

I keep telling myself I need to slow down, I need to be patient, but this is Hannah, and she is here, frantic, searching for comfort, searching for my body—her fingers tearing at the shirt she yanks from my body, her breaths hot and heavy against my chest.

In the yellow light, her skin glows. I wrench her hands from my body and pin them to the wall above her head, my other hand yanking at her pants, lowering just enough to allow me access before fumbling with my own.

I free my hard cock and guide it to Hannah's opening. She's soaked. The fear, the frenzy, the need all culminating in her desperation for me. And I know I should stop, or slow down but I can't, my need for her is all consuming, my desire a burning inferno that has me pulling her underwear to the side, and in one harsh buck of my hips I am inside her. We groan together, as if we are one being. A crazed depraved animal.

My naked chest crashes against hers, my hips piston into her wet pussy and I fuck her hard. There is nothing gentle here, nothing beautiful, none of the tenderness I wanted for our first time together again. There is only chaos.

Her mouth crashing into mine, her fingernails furrowing into my back, leaving long searing trenches. Her legs coil around my body, her hips answering mine, our breaths broken and heavy.

This isn't about pleasure, it's all about need, the need for human connection, to know that we are anchored to one another, that despite the isolation we are here together.

Hannah's keening sounds drive me on. Her soaking pussy

engulfs my cock as I thrust into her, sparing her nothing. The edge comes hurtling towards me like an avalanche breaking free, tumbling inside me violently, pleasure building frantically in the back of my spine before I explode inside her, fingers tugging her hair, teeth locked onto the skin of her collar bone, body jerking and her broken moans drowning me.

We still.

My forehead rests against her collarbone, now bearing the faint indent of my teeth. Her chest is frantic beneath me, rising and falling against mine, her skin slick with a sheen of sweat. Slowly, we untangle, her legs releasing me as I set her weight down, feeling the tremor in her muscles.

My gaze rests on the floor beneath us. I'm not ready for what I might see if I look up at her. I stare at the scuffed lines and old stains, like if I look hard enough, I'll find something there that explains what we just did. There's nothing. Just the hum in my blood and the taste of her still in my mouth.

She shifts slightly and the movement has me sucked back to the moment. I look up before I can stop myself.

I catch her gaze; there's no flinch, no retreat. Just something raw and unshielded that makes my whole body feel too tight. Our breaths still quickened, I lean down, and this time the kiss is soft. Slow, deliberate, laced with a different kind of need. A longing. An ache.

When we part, the silence is heavier than the pounding still emanating from outside. It's not awkward, exactly, just dense. Loaded. A wall has fallen between us, and there's no stepping around it anymore, only through it.

Her mouth parts, almost like she's about to speak, but the words snag somewhere in her throat. My own voice feels lodged there, too, thick with things I can't say.

"You okay?" It comes out quieter than I mean it to, but the question hangs in the air like smoke.

She dips her chin once, automatic, empty. "I don't know," she murmurs after a beat. "I just... can't stop hearing it in my head."

I know she's not talking about us. Not entirely. But my heart trips anyway.

"Then don't think about it," I murmur, though I'm not sure if I'm talking to her or myself. My thumb traces the inside of her wrist, slow, grounding. "Just... stay here. With me."

Her eyes lock on mine, searching, like she's weighing whether that's a promise or a trap. "And if I can't?"

I cup her face, holding her still, not letting her look away. "Let me give you a reason to."

The distance between us shrinks again, not rushed this time, not desperate. Just inevitable.

21. The Last Man on Earth

07/11/2025

I lead Hannah to the mattress, gently laying her down, crawling above her. For a few endless seconds, I feel like that helpless, madly in love teenage boy who was awkward and unsure, when the prize was getting her naked as quickly as possible and being inside her. There were no orgasms for Hannah, not really, and definitely not at first. Even as I got more sure I still had no idea what I was doing, and once I'd finally learned what all of it meant, Hannah was long gone. I'd cringe wondering if I'd ever have another chance to make it up to her.

And now holding her here, I do. I get to rewrite this part for us also. And I intend on making it memorable; this time I know what it means. What's at stake, and most importantly, how to make a woman come.

Achingly slow I remove her pants and underwear, leaving her entirely exposed, entirely vulnerable, entirely mine. I take endless mental pictures, embedding every detail into my very core. Her tangled wild hair, the stretch marks that streak along her buttocks like tiger stripes, a long pink scar that runs the length of her stomach. I kiss the slight, rose-coloured trench that remains from her underwear elastic, running around her hips like the equator line circling the world. And she is my world.

"You're beautiful," I breathe out as my mouth begins to trace her skin, nipping and kissing as I make my way up to her nipples.

Her lips part in a quivering, breathy hum of pleasure as I take one into my mouth. I suck and nip at it, dragging it out with my teeth. Hannah's breath hitches, and she arches into me, urging me on. She grinds against my hardness, her body craving mine, but Hannah is the prize, and I have worked too hard and too long to rush again, to give in to temptation.

"Ethan," she whispers my name, and I think that I might die right here in the dark office with her body beneath me. I suck on her beautiful nipple and play with the other, drawing sweet keening sounds from her that shoot right to my cock.

She is breathless and flushed and I haven't even started feasting on her, barely an aperitif. This perfect wild creature, hair framing her flushed face, hard pink nipples shining with my saliva and her glowing skin under the yellow light. She is a marvel, and I burn for her, barely holding the line between wanting and restraint.

I take her hands in mine and once more pin them over her head, kissing her gently. Holding my hunger at bay, reassuring her with my patience, with my attention. I want to show her just how much I love her; just how much I care. But more than anything I want her to trust me.

My mouth is loath to leave hers, so instead I pepper kisses along her jaw, her neck, the lines of her collar bone, until finally clamping around her nipple. My free hand traces a line down her belly till my fingers sink inside her.

We groan in unison.

"You're so wet for me." She releases a ragged sound of pleasure and a spasm shoots through my core.

With my mouth nipping and sucking at her tender nipple, my fingers slide in and out of her rhythmically, my thumb teasing her clit.

Hannah's knees begin to shake, her breaths come in short, sharp gasps, and her body tightens beneath me as I assault her body. My eyes glued to her beautiful face as it contorts in pleasure.

"Ethan..." She whimpers.

Hannah begging, needing, aching, is the most exquisite sound I have ever heard. Which is why I pull myself away, fingers and mouth gone all at once.

"Not so quickly, not so soon." My voice fraught with desire and darkness.

"Ethan," she whines.

"Shsssss." If only she knew how much pain I'm in to give her so much pleasure. Every part of me ached for her, my need searing my inside, but I'm desperate to have more of her first.

I release her wrists and slide down along her belly, kissing the flushed skin, making my way to her beautiful wet pussy. "Spread your legs for me, Hannah." My words gravelly through the effort of mastering my beast.

Her eyes flicker to mine, she doesn't know this version of me, but she complies, a little.

"More." She spreads herself wide for me. "So beautiful." The words fall from me in a reverent whisper and the flush on her cheeks deepens.

I settle between her legs before my tongue lashes out, and I get my first taste of Hannah. She moans and the sound has me melting.

Taking my time I enjoy leisurely laps at her perfect pussy, slow calculated licks, like she might be a sweet treat. I am in no hurry as I suck at her swollen clit. Hannah tries to grind herself against me, force the pleasure from my tongue but each time she does, I stop and wait for her breathless pleas. Her frustration is almost as delicious as her need.

My pace never wavers, not even when her legs begin to shake, her pleas rise in pitch louder, and her nails dig into my scalp. I know what she needs, what she wants, but I'm not going to give it to her, not yet. In fact, as she begins grinding on my mouth, aching for more pressure, I pull away from her, licking my lips.

"Ethan, please," she begs, and the words sear me. She doesn't have to ask anymore, we're both about to get what we want.

"Shhh, don't move." My voice is urgent, hungry, loaded with warning.

I take in my handy work. Hannah splayed on the mattress looking up at me through the veil of her long lashes, her glazed eyes glued to my body, her face flushed, her pussy swollen and her breasts heavy. Needy, desperate and finally mine.

Pulling my pants down, a jolt slithers through me as her mouth falls in a satisfied 'o'. I stroke myself and fall to my knees, settling between her. I am so hard it hurts, but all this pain is worth it. Hannah is worth everything.

"You are so beautiful, Hannah," I say, as I slide my aching cock between her wet lips, my cock teasing her sensitive clit, drawing ragged gasps from her sweet mouth. My hands slither to her breasts and I pinch her nipples, rolling them between my thumb and forefinger as my cock becomes slicker with her juices.

"Fuck, Ethan." We both hear the desperate quiver in her voice, and still, I need to make it last longer, draw it out a little further, because the minute I relent, the minute I take her, *really* take her, I will have no more control of my actions, my senses, my reactions, and I need *this*. I need this to sate my years of hunger, my years of yearning. I'm paying Hannah back for punishing me by punishing her. And I don't care that she caused me pain, all I know is that right now she's writhing beneath me in pleasure, and it's all my doing, and I can't get enough. I am drunk on watching Hannah enjoy me playing with her body.

Her pleasure begins to build again, but in turn so does mine, no more games.

I line my cock up at her entrance and ever so slowly I slide into Hannah, letting her feel every inch of me till I'm inside her to the hilt. I groan at the feel of her heat, her wetness, and I hold myself there, pulsing inside her, drowning in sensation.

"Fuck, you feel so good," I croon, watching the red deepen across her body, the flicker of her eyes as she watches that place between us, the bite of her lower lip. My cock flinches inside her.

I thrust once cautiously, Hannah moans, the sound washing over me.

For a second, all I can do is stare at her, half-convinced the universe is playing some cruel trick, because there's no way this is real, no way she's laying beneath me, looking up at me like that, breathing the same air. My heart feels too full for my chest, too fragile to hold it all. The weight of her, of this, of everything crashing over me, is too much and not enough all at once. I'm breaking apart just trying to hold it together, because I'm terrified that if I move, if I breathe wrong, I'll wake up and she'll be gone.

I thrust again, watching my slick cock covered in Hannah's wetness, her breathy cry caressing my heated body, and then, I'm gone, into the careening nowhere, pounding into Hannah with such ferocity I fear I might break her. But she meets me thrust for thrust.

Hannah's moans cascade from her mouth with each of my savage movements. Her body quivers with need and desperation, and this time I won't steal it from her.

I need it, we both need it, desperately.

She grinds against me, seeking relief as my body pounds against hers. Her nails dig into my flesh, our harsh breaths eradicate the chaos outside and Hannah and I are the only people left in the world.

Hannah's body shudders then jolts as she screams out her release, her body quivers and convulses with the pulsating waves of ecstasy, milking my cock. Her arms reach for my ass and she pulls me deeper inside her, grinding harder, and with that I am undone. All her walls clamp and squeeze me, her heat envelops me and her nails dig into my ass., My head rears back and my spine bows as my body tightens like stone. My mind careens off the abyss. I live in this moment. It's this, only this. I've lost myself in her; I'm no one, I'm obliterated. There's only an ecstatic burning pleasure, and I am losing, lost, unmade.

I pulse inside her, and she squeezes me tight. It's not just pleasure that I feel, but for the first time in ten years, I'm fucking content.

I find air in my lungs as I slowly come back down to earth and we are back in the office under the glow of the

LED lights. I rest my forehead against hers, and her arms hook around me. I kiss her swollen lips, sweet and gentle before pulling out, leaving a hot wet trail as I do. I fall on my back and pull Hannah into me, kissing her tenderly.

I want to say the words, they burn my tongue as I bite them down. Instead, I kiss the place where her shoulder meets her neck, feeling her warmth against mine, breathing her in.

The world is gone and all there is is Hannah and me.

"Well," Hannah says, breaking the silence with a breath that still catches in the middle. "That was... different."

I let out a low laugh, still flat on my back, staring at the dark ceiling like it might explain how the hell my heart's still beating. "Different like... gourmet popcorn different? Or different like we just rewrote a couple chapters of human anatomy?"

She nudges me with her foot. "Different like... good," she says, after a pause. "Unexpected. But good."

I turn to look at her, hearing all the words she isn't saying—pretending I didn't get any better by being with other women. Her hair's a mess, her cheeks flushed, and she's watching me with that same mix of amusement and something quieter that turns my insides upside down.

I pull out the only weapon I have left to defend myself with—poor humour. "I think I blacked out for part of it," I murmur. "Might need a formal debriefing."

Hannah raises an eyebrow. "You want me to draw you a diagram?"

"Oh, definitely. Preferably with annotations."

She laughs, then goes quiet, the moment hanging between us like a flickering match, seconds before it blows out.

I shift closer, brushing my fingers along hers. "I keep

thinking I'm gonna wake up," Heat creeps along my neck as I let my fear leak out into the room. "That this is some messed-up dream I built for myself. Because you, this... feels like too much to ask for."

She doesn't move, but I feel her watching me. The weight of it. The way she hears what I'm not saying.

"I never let myself picture it," I go on, slower now. "Not really. I mean, I joked, I planned, I hoped... but deep down, I think I was always waiting for the moment it would fall apart. You'd change your mind. I'd screw it up. Something would go wrong. Because that's what happens when you want something this badly."

"It's okay," her fingers ghost my chin, "there's plenty of time for all that."

"Hey!" She giggles as I roll on top of her, pinning her down beneath me with a hand braced on either side of her head, my body flush against hers. My protest dies in my throat as my desire ignites, insatiable.

I don't even try to resist it. I capture her mouth with mine, hungry, greedy. I'm no longer trying to hide what I feel, what I want.

She answers just as fiercely, fingers threading into my hair, pulling me closer, closer, like she needs me just as much as I need her.

The world outside fades, slipping away like a half-remembered dream.

The metal groans one last time, settling into silence.

And all that's left is her, and the way she's holding onto me like she's never letting go.

22. Day 7

08/11/2025

The world is silent.

When I wake, it takes a second to register why everything feels so different. It's not just the stillness or the warmth at my side, it's that there's no pounding, no scraping, no glass trembling in its frame. Just quiet. Heavy and complete. Sometime overnight the emergency lights have turned back on and their dim light falls across the room in neon green.

Hannah shifts beside me, her back pressing into me. And then, she freezes.

So do I.

A beat of silence.

Another.

"Um. What is that...?" knowing full well what she's feeling.

I clear my throat. "I brought a friend for breakfast."

"Did you now?" She turns her head, slow and deliberate, until her eyes find mine in the dim light.

"Mm-hmm." Growing bolder. "In case you are not aware, we are in an apocalypse, and rations are running low."

Her tongue flickers out of her mouth, skating along her upper lip. I have no idea if she notices the gesture, but it has my already-hard cock swelling, the rush of blood, forcing it to bob against her naked ass.

"Did your cock just slap my ass?"

"A friendly slap." I hold back my grin. "One might even call it an encouraging tap."

"Encouraging tap?"

"From a concerned friend that would hate to see you hungry." I'm pushing my luck, but Hannah is here, laughing in my arms, and possibly entertaining the idea of having my cock in her mouth.

"I *am* feeling peckish." She bites her lower lip as if considering what to order off the menu. A ball of anxious energy knots in my stomach, anticipation nipping at my skin as she grinds herself against me. She turns and kisses my chest.

"You look famished," I manage through gritted teeth. "Vanishing before my eyes."

She tilts her head back slightly, her hair spilling across my arm. "You offering breakfast?" she murmurs, all faux innocence, feathering her fingers across my stomach.

My breath catches. "Breakfast of champions."

"Champions?" She slides lower, peppering hot kisses along my taut abdomen, and I bite down a groan.

"Only the best for you, baby." I try to sound playful but we both hear my voice fraying at the edges.

Hannah settles at the edge of the mattress, her sexy ass supported on the backs of her ankles before landing a soft kiss on the head of my cock. Then a swirl of her tongue. A breath.

My pulse stutters as I watch her with awe. She spends a few moments trailing her tongue over my shaft as though she has all day and I am her favourite treat, which she wants to make last forever.

A tremble spreads up my spine at her languid exploration of my cock. Her eyes are on me as she takes her time licking, kissing, and gently sucking. My fingers thread into her hair, guiding but not forcing.

A thousand versions of this image had flashed across my mind countless times, but this reality surpassed every fantasy I'd ever dared to imagine.

Wrapping her mouth around my cock, Hannah devotes herself completely to her task, drawing me further down her throat, relaxing and sucking me into her mouth till she gags. Her throat closing on the head of my cock sends jolts of pleasure ratcheting up my back. She keeps going, over and over, slow and steady, taking her time, allowing us both to enjoy it rather than sprinting to get me off.

With each movement, she pulls low groans from the back of my throat, edging me closer and closer.

My fingers tighten in her hair. "Hannah." my voice is tight, fraught with need. "Stop, I'm about to come."

Hannah's eyes dance in the yellow glow as she meets mine, a slow, knowing smile spreads across her glistening lips. "But you promised me breakfast."

Her answer crushes every ounce of thought from me, leaving only awe, and I let out a strained exhale as her mouth wraps itself around my cock once more. She works her mouth up and down, taking as much of me as she can, her other hand caressing my balls.

My body tightens, a silent scream catches in my throat,

spilling out of me in a low growl. My hips take on a life of their own, moving erratically, and my body stiffens. "Oh, fuck. Fuck, Hannah." My body stills, then jerks spasmodically, my fist tightening in her hair, almost ripping as I jerk again. My cum spills out of me and into the back of her throat. She uses her mouth to suck down hard and my body stutters, releasing the rest.

"Fuck," I say again, my hand going limp in her hair as I try to regain the capacity for speech.

Hannah is licking her lips, and I'm awed, stunned, aching for more, like I'm starving for it. I can't remember the last time I came like that. It doesn't feel like it's enough.

Hannah crawls back along the bed, stretching alongside me. There's a slow, sleepy smile on her lips that does something ridiculous to my insides. I run my hands along her naked body and kiss her. "Fuck, Hannah," I whisper into her nape, landing a kiss against her heated skin, "that was..."

"An excellent breakfast..."

🧟🧟🧟

We stay in the office. It makes sense; it's safe, quiet, and we've already got the basics in here. There's a shelf of snacks, bottles of water, a box of LED lanterns, and all the comforts we have set aside for ourselves over the past seven days. Outside the door, the mall sits in hushed suspension, but in here, the day unfolds slowly.

Time moves differently in this room.

It doesn't pass so much as stretch, languid and forgiving, like even the hours are giving us space to breathe. The chaos outside is distant now, like the world's gone still just for us. I catch Hannah searching the walls, straining her ears, listening for an onslaught that never comes.

I pull back just enough to search her face. "You okay?"

"Yeah... it's just so quiet out there." Her eyes dart back to the closed door.

"I know," I say, brushing my thumb over her cheek. "But nothing's getting to you while I'm here. Not now, not ever."

Her shoulders loosen, the tension easing with each stroke of my thumb. "Promise?"

"Promise." I kiss her again, slower this time, like I can tether her to this room, to me, and keep the rest of the world out.

Hannah stretches, arms above her head, her shirt riding up just enough to make my brain short-circuit before I drag my eyes back to her face. She catches me looking and gives a slow, knowing smile, then shifts closer, her head resting on the pillow beside mine.

"So," she says, her voice low and familiar, "what did I miss while I was out there doing grown-up things?"

I huff a laugh. "Define grown-up."

"Taxes. Lesson plans. Falling asleep at 9:30 on a Friday night. You know. Thrills."

I roll to my side, propped on an elbow. "Sounds exhausting."

She snorts. "Says the guy who went off and became a tabloid myth."

"You pronounced *legend* incorrectly." I flex my arms showing off my sculpted biceps.

"Pffft." She jabs my ribs and my smile slips a little.

"Icon?"

"Hardly."

"Hey, I'm definitely noteworthy."

"In some circles."

"Don't even pretend you're not in one of those or should I bring up your stalking again?"

She giggles then rolls her eyes dramatically. "I'm pretty sure we were talking about your adult choices."

"Do we have to?"

"Yes." She's firm but warm as she studies my face.

I inhale deeply and look away, not wanting to see the flinch of disappointment in her face as I speak about my wasted potential and education. "Not much to say if I'm being honest. Mostly my mother kept trying to set me up with glamorous firms and high stakes titles but the more she pushed the more I pulled away. Instead of focusing and earning my own way, I played around like an idiot, hurting her reputation was the only way to get back at her."

"What for?"

I give Hannah a loaded look. "I think you know what for."

She takes my hand and squeezes, as if finally believing all the things I've been trying to explain to her for the last few weeks. Like maybe my truth is finally sinking in. A knot of anxiety churns and stretches in my stomach as I think about the truth.

"The reality is that I spent a lot of time on hidden beaches or in glossy cities; the kinds of places people chase like they'll fix something. I thought if I made enough noise, maybe I'd find a version of myself I didn't hate. I've spent most of the last ten years working out how to adult. Figuring shit out, you know?"

She looks at me like she sees through every word. "Did you?"

"Nope. Ended up right where I started. Just with a fancier suitcase and a lot more reasons to be disappointed in myself."

Hannah shifts again, the faint rustle of her shirt on the

mattress oddly comforting. "That's not nothing, you know. Coming home."

I don't answer right away. Her voice settles into the air like sunlight filtered through dust, warm and familiar. "I know." I give her a meaningful look and red creeps along her face.

"You'll do a lot of good here." She says it like she means it and my insides twist.

"I'm going to try." And I mean it.

I do want to make things better in Valenwood; build a legacy that's worth remembering. But in order to do that, I need to get out of here tomorrow, make the meeting, accept my role. And I need to tell Hannah everything.

And I will, but not yet... I shift the conversation back to Hannah, letting her talk.

She's telling me something about her first class, a kid who bit someone over a crayon, the way her colleagues all eat the same sad sandwiches at lunch like a silent pact. I'm listening. Sort of.

Her voice mellows around the edges when she mentions certain kids, certain stories. Her hands move when she's excited. Her mouth twists when she's thinking hard, and I get completely stuck on the shape of it. Her hair's messier than usual, a strand falling across her cheek, and I want to brush it back but don't. There's something sacred about just watching her, this version of her, grown and steady, yet still somehow the same girl who used to stomp through puddles just because I told her not to.

Same heart. Same spark. Just... more.
"Ethan?"
I blink. "Sorry, what?"
She grins. "You totally stopped listening."

I groan, covering my face. "I was listening. I just got distracted by... your face."

"Oh, my face, huh?" she deadpans.

"Mm hmm." I breathe. Slowly, stroking my chin like I'm about to deliver a TED Talk on the dangers of facial distraction. "Yep. It's *very* distracting. Moves around a lot. Does all these expressions. Impossible to focus."

She raises a brow. "My face moves?"

I nod, eyes transfixed on her mouth, the trace of a smile pulling at mine. "Mostly your mouth. Constantly. Very distracting. Frankly, it's a menace."

"You had no complaints about it this morning."

"None, zero, zilch, baby, in fact that's the kind of distraction I'll be willing to endure all day."

"Shocker."

"That's not a no." I smirk.

"Begging is just sad."

"I'm not begging, just stating a fun fact."

"Fun fact?"

"Mm hmm." My knuckles trace the line of her chin, "Fact is, I have a lot of fun with you, Hannah."

"And?" She leans in, lips brushing against my jaw.

"And I really, *really* like being distracted by your mouth."

She licks her lips and meets my gaze with feigned innocence, as if she has no idea what she's doing. "I'm glad you had fun, but alas, I'm afraid it was a temporary lapse in judgment."

"Sure," I say, voice low now, my hand trailing lightly down her back. "You planning to recover soon?"

She hums, shifting closer so there's barely anything between us. "That depends."

"On?"

"If you stop talking."

I do.

Right then.

Because suddenly her mouth is on mine, hot, certain, devastating. The air shifts, thick with heat and want. I kiss her back like she's the answer to every ache I didn't know I had, the balm to every wound I didn't realise I was carrying. Her fingers tangle in my hair, tugging just enough to let me know she's choosing me all over again. My hands slide to her waist, her hips, pulling her closer. Everything narrows to this, her lips, her breath, her body pressed to mine, until there's nothing left but the rush of her and the way she makes me feel.

I stretch out on the inflatable mattress, shifting to get comfortable. Hannah hums beside me, her fingers tracing lazy circles on my chest. We've spent the day tangled in one another, falling into easy conversations and even easier silences, getting reacquainted with the new versions of ourselves, filling in the quiet spaces the years have carved out between us.

The floor around us is a mess, empty water bottles, candy wrappers, a half-eaten bag of something neither of us can identify. The room has become a kind of quiet time capsule; the slow passage of the day etched into every corner.

My stomach growls—loudly—and Hannah lifts her head off her hand, one eyebrow arched.

"Again?" she says, the corner of her mouth twitching.

"Hey, I've been working up an appetite."

"Yes, yes you have," she murmurs with a sly grin, then giggles as I groan dramatically.

I roll off the mattress and lean over the low shelf where we've stashed the snacks. My hand closes around a bag of popcorn, and I hold it up like I've found treasure.

"That's a healthy dinner choice." She puts on her teacher voice, crossing her arms, watching me with mock judgment as I flop back down beside her and tear the bag open.

"Only the best for us," I say, mouth already half full.

I hand her the bag, and she plucks a piece from the bag and pops it into her mouth. "If this is the best, we're in trouble."

I shrug. "Come on, it's a complete meal."

She raises an eyebrow in a silent question.

"Vegetable—corn—check. Meat—BBQ flavouring—check. Salt—sodium—check. Add in air and some science and it's magic in your mouth."

She snorts. "Yeah, I've seen the kind of magic you put in your mouth."

"As have I," I jab back and she feigns shock as her cheeks flush with red.

"You really want to go there?"

"I mean, if you want to eat the same thing you did for dinner as you had for breakfast..."

She huffs theatrically, narrowing her eyes, and snatches a kernel, flicking it at my forehead. "You're lucky you're cute."

I crack a smile, swiping the bag back dramatically. "And you're lucky I'm willing to share."

"Your healthy meal in a bag?"

"An entire apocalyptic experience, popcorn and a show..."

"Mmm, yeah. Your clown routines are unforgettable."

I grab at my chest. "You wound me."

"I think you'll survive."

"Planning on giving me mouth to mouth?"

"You'd do anything to get my lips on you."

"Just about." I flash her my teeth and shove a handful of popcorn into my mouth before I say anything else.

We fall into another round of light jabs and popcorn theft, tossing kernels at each other until the bag lays empty on the floor beside us. Hannah curls against me, her head tucked beneath my chin, fingers grazing my ribs absently.

And all I can think is... this is it. This is all I ever wanted.

Just her.

Like this.

But even in the middle of perfect, I feel it rising again, that weight in my chest.

I have to tell her.

I lean against the pillow and stare at the ceiling, trying to find courage amidst that blank white wall, searching for the words I've been holding in all day. I know she deserves the truth, we both do, but the thought of her reaction tightens my throat, like a fist has closed around it.

I swallow hard and shift slightly, enough that she looks up at me.

"Hannah," Dread climbs up my throat. "There's something I need to tell—"

"That sounds serious," she interrupts before I can finish, studying my face, her eyes full of warmth. "And today has been such a good day, hasn't it?"

"The best day," I whisper.

"Then can it wait till tomorrow? I mean it's not like it really matters anymore... with the world having ended and all." She laughs that half-hearted laugh we all fall into in broken situations.

I manage a grimace, but it's a bad cover for the gnawing feeling in my stomach. "Yeah... sure, it can wait."

She puts her head back down and I listen to her breathing change as she drifts to sleep, leaving me with a heavy silence, her body pressed to mine, and the truth burning a hole in my chest. Because for the first time in forever, I have everything I've ever wanted... and I've never been closer to losing it.

23. Making my own bed

10/10/2025

Standing at the podium in the town hall, the collective gaze of Valenwood pins me in place, heavy and relentless. The room is packed, every seat filled, with a few people standing in the back. The familiar faces of Valenwood peek out from the crowd, watching me like I might set the place on fire just for the fun of it.

Their resentment is palpable. Sons always pay for the sins of their fathers. I haven't lived here or been involved in the town for years, steering clear of my father's business. But now, with his death, the universe has forced me back here, and I'm stuck.

If I'm going to fix things, I have to start with the most important thing.

Hannah.

All I have to do, is convince a room full of people who hate me, to help.

I've brokered million-dollar deals before, so this should be easy. At least that's what I tell myself, forcing a breath. Then I look out at them, at the crossed arms, the unimpressed stares, and I realise 'easy' is a term reserved for first-year law graduates trying to sway a jury that's already made up its mind.

"Thank you all for coming," I start, my voice steady despite the minefield detonating in my stomach. "I know you're wondering why I called this meeting, so I won't waste your time. I need your help to bring about the end of the world."

Silence.

Then laughter.

Loud, brash, incredulous. People shake their heads, whisper to their neighbours, some openly jeer.

Frank, of course, is the first to caw from the back. "Oh, this ought to be good. How much did he inherit again? Maybe he's lost his damn mind."

I let the moment stretch, then lift my chin. "I'm not joking. I need Valenwood to become the epicentre of a worldwide catastrophe. A place lost to time, cut off from civilisation, where nothing and no one can get in or out. We are going to stage the end of the world. And I need all of you to help me do it."

Murmurs ripple through the room, the laughter fading into something wary.

"You want to shut the town down?" Dave Thompson, the local mechanic, squints at me like he's searching for the crack in my skull that let this idea out.

"Yes," I slice the air with my hand for emphasis.. "I need you all to act like the world has ended. And more specifically, I need you to act like zombies."

That sets them off again. The room erupts with laughter, some shaking their heads, others outright muttering about me wasting their time. But I stand there, waiting. Eventually, they start quieting, realising I'm not joking.

"Why?" Helen Fisher, the owner of the only hair salon in town, demands from the back, voice sharp. "Why would we do that?"

"Because it'll be worth your while. Think of it as a paid vacation in the strangest theme park imaginable. No bills, no daily grind. Just a little... theatre."

A few people frown, considering it. Others still look unimpressed.

"And how, exactly, are we supposed to survive if you're shutting everything down?" Barry Walker, the pub landlord leans in, arms crossed over his broad chest. His two shadows, Frank and Rob, sit on either side of him, a three-headed serpent ready to strike.

"The town's trade will continue," I assure them. "Online orders will still be processed through the storage facilities. Supplies will still be delivered. Your businesses will not suffer. No one will lose money. But for anyone living here, inside Valenwood's borders, the world will be over. To anyone looking in, this town will be lost."

That gets their attention. They shift, glancing at one another.

"Why on earth would we do that?" shouts Mrs. Jenkins from the back, her tone laced with scepticism. "This some kind of joke?"

"No joke," My fingers grip the edges of the podium, knuckles blanching. "I have my reasons, and while I can't share all the details, I promise it's important. I just need everyone to go along with it."

They're all still murmuring, wading in suspicion like fading swimmers. I push on. "All you need to do is go about your daily lives, but as zombies. Groaning, shuffling, and generally acting like you're the living dead. But, and this is important, you must not break character until I give the signal. And one more thing," I look around the room meeting as many eyes as I can, "Hannah Jones is not to be informed of any of this. This is crucial."

Fiona pushes to the front, her eyebrows knitting together. "Hannah? What does she have to do with this?"

"I need her to believe it's real."

A fresh ripple of whispers spreads through the crowd. Frank stands abruptly, his chair scraping against the floor. "This is absolutely insane!" His voice is strangely high-pitched, and he clears his throat before continuing. "You want us to trick a girl? For what, some sick joke?"

"It's not like that," he lets out a derisive laugh ending my protest.

"Oh, it's exactly like that," Rob cuts in. "And you expect us to go along with it? You waltz back into town, throwing money around like it fixes everything."

Barry grunts, arms folded tight. "We're not fools just because we live in Valenwood. What's in this for you?"

My grip on the podium tightens. "I know it sounds ridiculous, but this is bigger than just me. And yes, maybe I am throwing money at the problem, but at least I'm offering something in return. Compensation. I only need one week, and I promise that you'll earn more in those seven days than you would in double the time at your day job, with the added benefit of retaining your paid time off."

I'm greeted with murmurs and head shakes.

"I'm asking for one week." It's all I have, it's all I can afford to take. Hannah's parents go off for their Parisian trip on the first week of next month, not to mention my meetings with the board and the lawyers. If I don't legally take my father's place, things will start falling apart. The board meeting is scheduled for the Monday after that week. Missing it isn't an option. My mother would have my balls in a noose for the rest of my life if I skipped it. I have my own money, sure, but she knows how to make everything a misery.

"It's not going to work you know." Fiona doesn't raise her voice; she doesn't have to, it cuts through the noise like a blade and suddenly everyone in the room understands, and the full spectrum of my own pathetic existence washes over me; desperate, deluded, reckless, standing here trying to buy the end of the world like it's just another business deal. Trying to buy Hannah's love back. For a second I contemplate walking out—leaving it all behind—the town, the idea, the pitiful looks and cackling laughter.

I open my mouth to argue, then shut it again, realising I have nothing left to trade but desperation. A hot flush crawls up my neck, my shoulders sag and my head bows, the weight of my own absurdity pressing me down. I stare at the scuffed wood beneath my feet wishing that board would swallow me whole.

But just then, she says it, sending my heart lurching from my chest. "I'll do it."

My head snaps up and our eyes lock across the room. The look she gives me is disappointed. Not angry, not surprised, just a quiet, tired disappointment. I don't know if she's disappointed in me for asking or in herself for agreeing. Maybe both. Maybe neither. Maybe she just needs the money, money she only needs because she gives too many free coffees to people who need them more than her.

Fiona's words opened a fault line and now the tremor is running through the room, the others start to shift in uneasy agreement. Even the sceptics. Even the three-headed beast in the back, though Frank and Rob grumble the whole time.

And as Fiona steps forward to sign the NDA my lawyers thought was proof of my insanity, the tension in my spine loosens.

I did it.

The plan is in motion.

And yet, my insides constrict. Because now, I actually have to go through with it.

24. Convincing Bruce and Laura

11/10/2025

"No!"

"Please, just hear me out."

We're on the back deck of my mother's house, the only place I could think of that Hannah wouldn't stumble across us or hear about this meeting.

It's quiet, tucked away behind the main house and hidden from the road. The long wooden table is polished smooth in the centre, and a crystal carafe filled with chilled water lays untouched, next to the small stack of manila envelopes. Beyond the railing, Valenwood stretches out in a blur of low stone walls and trimmed hedges, but the world feels far away here. Private. Controlled.

Laura sits across from me in her signature black attire; she's tense like an unsheathed blade. Her eyes haven't softened since the day I saw her in the street, playing human shield between Hannah and me. The memory flickers, sharp and unwelcome.

Bruce is wedged in the chair beside her, hunched and rigid, arms folded across his chest like a barricade. He doesn't speak, but his silence is loud, his hatred simmering under the surface, directed entirely at me. Not just for what I did to Hannah, but for ever having her in the first place. For throwing her away. For having everything he ever wanted and never got.

My lawyer sits to the side, briefcase open, lips pressed in a line. He's here to witness the signatures and my stupidity.

"No! Whatever it is, if it's about Hannah I don't want to hear it, you'll just hurt her again."

"I won't.'"

"You will. Nothing's changed, you're still a Vale and she's still... *uncivilised.*"

Her tone stings but I keep my face schooled and my emotions in check. There is too much at risk to get into a fight with Laura; she is probably the one person this entire ridiculous plan hinges on.

"Those were my mother's words."

"You didn't correct her."

"I was young and stupid."

"And if you think I'm going to help you then the only thing that's changed about you is that you're no longer young."

Bruce's mouth twitches in that smug little way when he thinks he's won, but I don't care, let him think what he will, I'm ready for all her rebuffs.

"I'll pay for your wedding."

She stills, pupils blown wide as she freezes, staring at me.

"Wherever you want to host it, with as many guests, everything you ever dreamt of, the dress, the catering, the destination, on me."

"Laura..." Bruce chimes in, watching as a spark flickers in her eyes.

She sits across from me, her fingers nervously tapping the coffee cup, her engagement ring clanking against the porcelain. Bruce shakes his head and stands up, making his way to the far wall that looks over the town.

Laura glances up at me, studying my face. I lean back in my chair, trying to appear calm and patient, though the tension in the air bites my skin.

"Why? Why now?"

"Because I still love her, because I've wasted enough time, because now I can offer her what I couldn't before."

"Wouldn't."

"It was complicated."

"It wasn't."

"I had no choice."

"Of course you did, you just chose wrong."

"Fine." I know what Laura thinks of me, I know what they all think of me—but they don't know who I am and what Mother is really like. I draw a calming breath. "What's your choice then?" I'm out of patience and out of time, I'm tired of getting punished for being a stupid kid put in a shitty situation. I wasn't even all to blame; she didn't even give me a chance. "Telling Hannah or having the perfect wedding?"

She bites her lip. "What you're asking... It feels... wrong."

I lean forward, trying to bridge the gap between us with my sincerity. This is it. I have to win Laura over. If she caves, Bruce will have no choice; she won't let him ruin her dream. "I know how much you love Hannah, how much she means to you, but you have to understand that despite everything, I love her too. And all I want is a chance to speak to her, clear the air, apologise, give her my side of things."

"So take her out to fucking dinner like a normal person."

"I've tried; she had me arrested."

Laura's mouth stretches into a knowing smile. "Yes, I know."

Her fingers stop tapping, and she irons out her skirt with her palms, exhaling deeply. Her gaze ping-pongs between Bruce, who shakes his head, and the NDA tucked in a folder on the table between us, indecision pooling in her expression like dark water.

"Can I at least have some time to think about it?"

"No. I have a deadline. Her parents are going out of town next month and she'll be home alone."

"How do you kno—"

I hold my hand up to stop her. "Yes or no, Laura, I have things to do."

"You're putting me in an impossible situation."

"Yeah, been there..." A flicker of hatred slices through her features.

Her mouth tightens as she gives the barest dip of her head, expression pinched, as though she's swallowing poison. "Okay, I won't say anything." She's already reaching for the pen.

"Laura!" Bruce's head whips around and his stare widens.

"Bruce, you have to do this for me."

"Are you fucking insane? We're not doing this!" His words drip of venom, his arctic eyes piercing through me.

"But he'll pay for my wedding, everything. You know how long I've been wanting this."

"But it's Hannah, we have—"

"Bruce." She stands and takes a small step in his direction. Pushing up on her tip toes, she closes a hand over his ear her words muffled as she speaks. His face loses colour, and his eyes grow wide the longer she talks. When she steps back, he lets his head drop for a second before looking up at Laura.

"Fine," he says, his eyes locked on hers, anger burning behind them. They keep staring at each other, the pregnant silence strained. "Fine," he says again, hands coming up in surrender before he pushes away from the wall, grabs the pen from the table and scribbles his name violently on the dotted line before slamming the pen down and stalking away.

I tilt my head towards Laura, arching an eyebrow, the question unspoken between us.

"He won't say anything."

I hold her gaze. "Thanks, Laura."

She skewers me with an icy stare. "Not like you gave me a choice. I'm never going to like you."

"I know."

"If you hurt her again..."

"That's not what I want—"

"Have you ever bothered to think about what Hannah wants? Maybe she doesn't want to talk to you again. Maybe you should just respect her wishes."

I nod but disagree. "Guess there's only one way to find out."

"Let's not talk again." She cuts me off and storms out.

I watch as she trudges through the lounge. Martha will find her and lead her out. I know I've put her in a difficult position, but if Hannah will only talk to me if the world ends then that's what I need to do.

25. The truth

08/11/2025

I wake up tangled in my dreams and reach for Hannah just to discover she is no longer in my arms. I jolt up, and for a long moment consider that maybe I dreamt it all. Her deafening smile, her exquisite mouth, our groping hands and gasping breaths. But one glance down on my naked body, tells me it was real.

Laying back the memories spool across my mind reliving every inch of Hannah inside my mind. I barely remember falling asleep, but I remember her, warm against me, entwined and safe.

I slip on my underwear and jeans and make my way to the bathroom, grinning to myself. My hair's a mess, a chaos of dark waves, and I look ridiculous with this stupid, unstoppable grin.

Turning on the tap, I splash cold water on my face, the shock jolting me awake. I run a wet hand through my hair and down my face, wiping away any trace of sleep. Toothbrush. Foam, a mouthful of water to rinse out that morning taste.

When I lift my head, the mirror shows me empty space where she should be, but her warmth still clings to me. My core tightens at the thought.

I wipe my face, exhaling in a laugh. It's like my chest is too small for this feeling. This is insane. But beneath that rush, there's something else, something colder. I need to tell her the truth. Today. No more avoiding it. But for now, for a few more minutes, I want to hold on to this. To her.

I step back, my attention drifting to the partition between the stalls. Hidden there, tucked just out of sight, is the satellite phone. I stashed it there a few days ago knowing she wouldn't find it. Despite being the only two survivors of an apocalypse, we've given each other the privacy of separate male and female bathrooms.

Reaching for it, and power it on. The screen flickers to life and I start typing, my fingers moving fast.

Then, a scream.

Sharp.

Panicked.

"Ethan!" Her screech echoes in the empty mall, and I almost drop the satellite phone in my panic. I set it aside, balancing it on the partition between the stalls and rush out towards her.

Hannah stands near the glass door with two cups of coffee in her still hands, her silhouette rigid. I know that posture, the way her shoulders square like she's bracing for a fight.

I approach cautiously. "Hannah? What's wrong?"

She doesn't answer right away, her head tilting slightly as if straining to hear something. I edge closer, following her line of sight through the narrow gap in the barricade.

And then I see it.

Two 'zombies' loitering just outside the mall, completely out of character. One is leaning against a car, cigarette dangling lazily between his fingers, while the other devours a hot dog with an enthusiasm that borders on comedic. They're chatting. Laughing. Completely oblivious to the world-ending scenario they're supposed to be a part of.

I freeze.

"What the hell is going on?" Her gaze swings from Tom and Gary back to my face, and a knot form in the pit of my stomach.

"Hannah." I inch towards her, and her eyes lock onto mine, her face contorting and twisting as if she is trying to figure something out. "What?" But I already know what, even before she says it.

"You're not surprised..." She scrutinises my face.

"Wha—?"

"You. Are. Not. Surprised." She punctuates each word with a step toward me.

"Hannah," I try. Adrenaline shoots through my body as it registers the danger. It's not anything outside I'm worried about. It's the danger of losing Hannah for good.

"What's happening right now?" Her eyes glint with unshed tears, her face marred with confusion.

"Hannah."

"No more lies, Ethan."

All the air leaves my lungs as my pulse slams into over-drive, hammering in my chest, in my throat, in my ears. Every instinct screams at me to play it cool, to school my face into something neutral, but It's too late. My body betrays me; too stiff, too still, too obviously wrong. And then there's the waiting. That unbearable, stretched out second when it's clear she already knows.

"We faked it." I blurt it out.

"We... Faked? We..." She swallows half the word as she pants out, reality slamming into her. "Faked it? Everyone?" Her broken voice cleaves through me, pouring guilt into my body. She's already retreating and I try to follow.

"Hannah."

She throws the coffee in my direction, the boiling water narrowly missing me. "Stay away from me!" Her brittle voice spears me.

She backs away, her face contorted with anguish and confusion, her breath coming in short sharp pants, her world spinning out of control.

Again.

She backs into the camping shop and vanishes.

I slump against the wall, my stomach hollow and twisted like I've missed a step on the stairs, but worse, because there's no catching myself. No fixing it. Just the crushing, skin-prickling awareness that I've been caught.

When my legs feel solid again, I make my way back to the bathroom. Each step a slog, as though I am walking through water. I grab the phone, my message still half-typed in the box, deleting it, I start again.

'She knows.'

I stare at the screen until finally three dots dance around.

'Was bound to happen, sweetheart.'

Not helpful at all. But then I shouldn't have expected more; she isn't wrong.

'What do I do?'

The dots appear and disappear a number of times, my frustration growing with each ticking second.

When the answer finally comes, it's not what I want to hear.

'I don't know, you'll have to figure that part out on your own.'

My fingers fly over the keyboard in frustration. What does she mean she doesn't know—what kind of friend is she? I need her help, advice, anything.

My fingers slow with every keystroke, until they stop entirely, leaving me gaping at the jumble of words on the screen. As always, Sookie is right—I dug this hole, I need to find a way to get myself out.

I delete the insane paragraph and text her back.

'You're right.'

'I know. You doing ok?'

'Not sure.'

'We'll be here when you get out.'

'Thanks.'

The phone sits quiet in my hand, screen blank. Seems as if Sookie's said all she is going to.

A few minutes later I gather myself and return to the camping shop, weaving around the aisles, staying hidden. I want to go to her, to somehow make this all better, but instead, I sink to the floor like a coward, hidden behind the laden shelves, and listen to her savage cries as they fill the space with her sorrow.

�✢✦✦✛✢

I wake to the sounds of crashing trollies and breaking pot plants. I scramble to my feet in the darkness and fumble my way to the large glass doors that we barricaded.

Hannah is there, brutally and systematically dismantling it.

My approach is cautious. Each step toward her feels like I'm walking barefoot over broken glass; slow, careful, knowing I'll bleed for it but unable to stop myself. My chest tightens, my breathing too shallow, and the closer I get, the worse it gets, like something inside me is bracing for impact.

She's a wreck. Eyes red-rimmed and puffy, smaller somehow, fragile even though I know she's not. There's something broken about her—and I was the one who broke it. The sight of her knocks the air from my lungs.

I force my hands to stay loose at my sides, resisting the urge to run to her, to reach for her, to gather her up in my arms and fix this world I broke for her—again. But of course that would be the worst thing I could do right now. Instead, I swallow against the lump in my throat and take another step, softer this time, careful not to startle her.

Her body stiffens before she even looks at me. Like she can sense me. And when she finally does lift her head, when those exhausted, furious eyes lock onto mine, it's like the ground beneath me drops out.

"What the hell do you want?" Her voice is steeped in venom. Her hands get back to work as if, despite her speaking to me, I'm not even there.

My mouth is dry. My pulse is a wild, erratic thing in my chest. I want to say her name, want to start with something —anything that makes this less unbearable. But my voice feels rusted over, my throat tight, because I know whatever I say next has to matter.

"Can we talk?" The question sounds pathetic even to me, and I hate myself for asking it—those were not the words to approach her with.

"What about?" she spits out while flinging another trolley out of the way. It crashes into another and they rattle loudly.

"Let me explain…"

"You mean lie to me some more?"

My hands knot into tight balls at my sides. "I deserve that but it's not—"

"Not what it looks like?" she snaps, cutting me off, her eyes blazing like twin infernos. "Because it looks a hell of a lot like you've been lying to me. From the very beginning."

I try to reach for her, but she steps back, her hands clenched around another loose trolley that she hurls in my direction, forcing me to step back and aside. "How long, Ethan? How long were you planning to keep this up? Until I lost my mind? Until I begged you to make it stop?"

"It's not like that," I blurt out, desperation clawing at my throat. "I swear, I didn't know—"

"How gullible I am? How far you could take it? How long you could traumatise me for and see how far I'd fall for it?"

"No!" I shout, the word echoing through the empty mall. "It's not like that….'

"Stop saying that!" Her scream is shrill and full of annoyance, punctuated by another trolley barrelling in my direction.

"I was trying to fix things. To fix *us*."

She stares at me, incredulous. "Fix us? You call this fixing? Do you have *any* idea what you've done to me? You made me believe the world was *gone*, Ethan. That everyone I've ever known is dead!"

"I thought—"

"No, you didn't think!" she yells, her words splintering. "You didn't think about me, about how this would affect me. You only thought about yourself. About whatever twisted logic made you think *this* was okay."

"I didn't mean to hurt you."

"But you did," she snaps. "You don't get to decide what's best for me, Ethan. You don't get to play God with my life!"

I try to step closer, but she backs away, shaking her head. "You manipulated me," Her words fracture, sharp and uneven. "You used my fear against me, and for what? To what end, Ethan?"

"I've always told you I would love you till the end of the world, and you said the same to me." The confession rasps out of me. "I wanted to give us that chance, to be the last people left on this earth. I wanted to talk to you again, to make you laugh again, to remind you of what we had. I just wanted us to be us again."

She glares at me, her expression twisting into something between anger and heartbreak. "But the world didn't end, Ethan, you just fucking lied. You don't fix things by breaking someone's trust."

Her words feel like daggers, each one finding its mark.

Hannah turns away, her fingers twitching, grip unsteady as she yanks at the chains holding the doors closed, the last semblance of the barricade that kept us together.

"Hannah, don't. Please—"

She spins back around, fury and hurt warring across her face. "I never ever want to see you again, Ethan."

I'm frozen, helpless as the heavy metal chain clatters to the ground and she pushes the doors open. Cold night air rushes inside, pushing aside the stale warm air we have been breathing for the last week.

Outside, three figures lurk in the shadows. Their heads snap toward her as she steps outside, and they charge—Frank taking the lead.

Hannah stands her ground, not moving at all, and as

Frank rushes at her, she flinches for a moment, as if still uncertain of what's real and what's not, before she punches him full in the face. Barry and Rob freeze in place.

Frank stumbles back groaning, his hand shooting to his face. "Oouuww."

Hannah's jaw twitches and locks as she looks at each man in turn, taking in their elaborate makeup and distorted features. "Really? I would have expected this from him," her head flicks in my general direction, "but not you guys." She sounds so fucking disappointed.

"Hannah..." all three call after her in unison, but she's already walking through the parking lot and away from us.

I don't even have the strength to follow. All I can do is watch as she disappears into the night, the weight of her anger and disbelief crushing me where I stand.

The three men step closer, shoulders squared, arms crossed. Their eyes lock on me, hard and unblinking, and a low, tense silence hangs between us, and now I have a whole new problem to deal with.

26. When only friends and alcohol will help

Two months later - 13/01/2026
Ethan

The whiskey burns going down, but I don't stop. I keep tipping the glass back again, letting the slow, creeping warmth spread through me. The room around me is dimly lit, the glow from the kitchen casting long shadows. Somewhere in the background, Angie hums as she washes dishes, Sookie sits across from me, her sharp eyes tracking my every move.

Their house is small but lived-in, a stark contrast to the sprawling emptiness of my father's estate. The furniture is mismatched, the walls covered in a collage of photos; family, friends, moments frozen in time. It smells like coffee and vanilla, like comfort, but none of it reaches me.

"You look like shit," Sookie finally says, breaking the silence.

I snort, swirling the amber liquid in my glass. "And yet, still not the worst I've ever looked."

She doesn't argue. Instead, she leans back in her chair, crossing her arms. "So, she still won't talk to you?"

I huff out a bitter laugh. "Talk? She won't even stay on the same side of the street as me. I've tried every possible way to reach her. Calling from multiple numbers—all blocked within minutes. Messaging from different social media accounts—ignored without hesitation. Showing up at her door, at her friends' doors, only to have them slam it shut in my face. Her mother was the only exception. She didn't slam the door. She looked at me with pity which was so much worse than the anger. Then there were the flowers she threw from her window, and the boxes of gifts she discarded unopened, but not before she completely demolished them first." I swirl what's left in my glass, watching the amber spiral like it might give me answers.

"Honestly, I would have given the world's best stalkers a run for their money. And still, nothing. She's gone underground. The whole damn town is pretending I don't exist."

Sookie's gaze sharpens.

"Has she tried to have you arrested again?"

I shake my head, rubbing my temple.

"No, but I'm genuinely surprised she hasn't tried to have me framed for murder."

Angie snorts from the sink, drying her hands on a rag. "She doesn't need to. Pretty much anyone in town would happily do it for her."

And that's the thing, isn't it? It's not just Hannah avoiding me, it's everyone. The entire town is acting strange. The same people who signed the NDAs and agreed to my insane plan are now walking around like ghosts themselves, guilt simmering beneath the surface. They see me and immediately look away. They barely even look at each other.

Maybe they thought it was harmless at the time. Maybe they told themselves it was all just a bit of fun, a theatrical joke that comes with a wad of cash. But now, standing in the wreckage of it all, they know the truth: they helped me ruin her for money. Shame follows them around like a heavy robe.

They all helped me. They all played their part. But now that it's done, they don't know what to do with themselves. Neither do I.

In the end though, it's my name they spit out like a curse. I am the common enemy, the easy scapegoat, the bad guy. In time, she'll learn to forgive them all. She's known these people her entire life, they will worm their way back because Hannah is the forgiving type. She will see their logic, feel their pain and understand their moral dilemmas, she will believe I manipulated them, forced them, enticed them.

It's me she won't forgive.

I take another long sip, the alcohol burning less this time. My thoughts spiral, twisting back to the last time I was this drunk. The last time I let myself drown in it—with Hannah. That night at the bar, after Rob bit that man. Shit, that cost a small fortune. Not just to appease Rob for having to bite down on the man with a mouth full of fake blood that probably tasted like crap, but also to that family. Lawsuits are a messy thing and painting the sole heir of the Vale fortune a nut job is even costlier.

But we did get drunk, and I did get her laughing, eventually. Her voice slurred as she ranted about the Screwpocalypse. I snort as I think about her crazy theory. Angie and

Sookie exchange a look, then both turn to look at me with questioning expressions.

I close my eyes, tipping my head back against the chair. "I was just thinking about Hannah's screwpocalypse."

Angie frowns. "Look, what you got up to in that ma—"

"No. It's not like that—though I was also hoping it would be. The screwpocalypse…" A sharp, humourless laugh escapes me. "It was her theory about the end of the world, how screws hold everything together and a real apocalypse is when they all vanish overnight, and everything slowly breaks down piece by piece."

"Not what I was expecting." Angie's slanted smile lights up her face.

"Trust me, me either."

"Well one thing is for sure," Sookie says, grabbing a cigarette from the box and lighting it up.

"What's that?"

"You sure did screw yourself."

We all share a chaste laugh.

I swallow hard, my throat tight. "She said that if the world was ending, she'd rather not know it was coming. She wanted to go about her day, drinking her coffee, laughing at something stupid, and then—bam. Over."

The memory is so vivid I swear I can hear her laughter, smell the whiskey on her breath, feel the warmth of her leaning into me. And now, here we are. The world ended—at least for me. And she knew it was coming. I made sure of that.

My insides constrict. The room tilts slightly. Sookie is watching me too closely now, her lips pressing into a thin line so that the smoke flows out of her nose.

"This was your idea," I mutter, my words slurred,

accusatory. "You were the one who told me to do something big."

She doesn't flinch away, instead, she shrugs at my pathetic attempt to shift the blame. "Yeah. And you did. And now you know."

I blink at her. "Know what?"

She leans forward, resting her elbows on the table. "You and Hannah always said you'd love each other until the end of the world." Her tone remains steady, unwavering. "But clearly, she doesn't. So now you know. And maybe it's time you made your choice."

The words cut deeper than I expected. I stare at her, my heart hammering. I told her I'd love her until the end of the world. And I did. I ended it for her.

But she didn't choose me.

The nausea climbs up my throat. I reach for the bottle instead of my glass and pour another drink, my fingers shaking.

Angie sighs, coming over to the table, nudging my shoulder as she sits beside me. "Look. We get it. But at some point, you have to ask yourself what's left to fight for? You pulled off the impossible. The whole town went along with your crazy plan. You did everything to get her back. And she's still gone."

The truth of it is a sledgehammer to the chest.

I press my hands to my face, exhaling harshly. "I don't know how to let her go."

Silence settles between us. The clock ticks. The ice in my glass melts. Angie nudges the bottle away from me.

Sookie's tone is softer this time. "I know it's hard, but give yourself time and you'll find a way to move on."

Move on.

The words sound like a foreign language, something I'm

not sure I'll ever be able to translate. Because how do you move on when everything you built, everything you thought you knew, was tied to one person?

I glance between them, searching for something—an argument, an alternative, a way to fix this.

But there's nothing. Only the quiet truth of what's left.

I've lost her.

And now, I have to decide what comes next.

27. Decisions Decisions

22/01/2026

Hannah

I'm folding a pair of jeans when Laura barges in, holding two cups of coffee. She sets one down on the dresser. "Fiona sends her love."

"She can keep it," I mumble under my breath as Laura perches on the edge of my bed like she owns the place.

"Well, good morning, sunshine."

"I'm not in the mood today, Laura."

"You're never in the mood."

She sighs, and a part of me wants to suffocate her with my pillow.

"Yeah, sometimes that happens when you get tricked by every single person you know and get locked up in a mall with a crazy man thinking everyone you love is dead."

"Oh." She's nonchalant, but I do see her shoulders tense as I speak. "Still playing the 'my entire town faked an apocalypse so some guy I'm totally in love with got to spend some alone time with me' card?"

"Yeah, it's a pretty good card."

She takes a sip of her coffee, attempting to drown out the uncomfortable tension between us. I've tried to forgive Laura, to understand why she made the choices she did, but it's going to be a long time before I can trust her again—trust anyone, for that matter. It's a process. My therapist says that's normal. I have no idea what normal is anymore.

"Speaking of cards," she clears her throat, "I saw him yesterday, lurking outside Fiona's."

"Creeps do lurk."

"Says the crazy internet stalker."

"Shut up, that's not even remotely the same thing."

"Mm hmm, sure." She sniggers. "He looks like shit."

"Good. I hope he's suffering."

"Won't be for much longer."

At that my back stiffens, and my stupid heart flurries in my chest. "What do you mean?"

"Haven't you heard? He's leaving town. For good this time. He's officially on the board of the Vale group; he's moving to London or New York or something."

"Good riddance." The disappointment creeps into my voice, no matter how hard I try to fake indifference.

"Once he's gone, you'll never see him again."

"Perfect."

"You're being stubborn." She swivels to look at me.

I roll my eyes, stuffing a jumper into the drawer.

"I'm serious." She leans back, her arms braced against the bed. "The guy practically ended the world for you. You're acting like that's not a big deal."

Slamming the drawer shut a little harder than necessary, I grab another pile of clothes. "He lied to me. You lied to me. Everyone lied to me. Excuse me if I don't feel like swooning over his grand 'gesture'."

"It wasn't just a gesture; it was a masterpiece," she counters, taking a sip of her coffee. "Do you have any idea how much planning it must've taken? Fake zombies? A whole fake apocalypse? The logistics alone!"

I toss a shirt onto the bed. "Oh, wow. You're right. Let me fall to my knees in gratitude for the man who tricked me into thinking everyone I care about is dead."

"Hannah, come on." Laura stands and grabs a sweater from my pile, folding it neatly. "It wasn't just about the spectacle. It was about you. Ethan did all of that because he loves you. He wanted you back."

"And you helped him, even knowing how I feel about him." I snatch the sweater from her hands and shove it into the closet.

"Yes, I did, because I know exactly how you *really* feel about him."

We stare at each other for a brief second, but I'm not giving up my anger this easily. "Yes—I *really* feel that he is a lying piece of shit, who thinks he can buy anything and anyone—even you. I mean you did get a wedding out of it, didn't you?"

Laura sighs and flinches like I'd physically hurt her. For a second, my own heart squeezes with guilt, but just as quickly hardens again. I'm not to blame for any of this. "Okay, yes. But it's not like I didn't think it was insane. I mean, I told Ethan it was a terrible idea. But... it was also kind of brilliant."

"Brilliantly manipulative," I mutter, grabbing a pair of socks from the floor.

Laura shifts uncomfortably. "Hannah, I know you think I just went along with it like it was some big joke, but it wasn't like that. At first, I thought he was crazy. I told him to leave you alone, that it was too much. But he wouldn't listen. And then, somewhere along the way, I started thinking... maybe it could work. Maybe if you just saw how much he loved you—"

"Stop," I cut her off, my voice sharp. "Do you know what it felt like? To wake up every day thinking the world was over? To believe that my parents were dead? That my entire life was gone? And then to find out it was all a lie? That everyone I trusted was in on it? You think that's something you can just fix with 'but he loves you'?"

She recoils slightly, as if the words strike her skin, and I see the guilt settle in her eyes. "I—I didn't think about it like that. I swear. I never wanted to hurt you."

I exhale sharply and sit on the edge of the bed, my hands locked on my knees. "You were my best friend. And you let me believe it."

Laura hesitates before sitting beside me. "I know. And I hate that I hurt you. I hate that you won't look at me the same way anymore. I messed up, babe. But... so did he. And I'm not saying you have to forgive him. I just... I need you to know that he didn't do it to hurt you. He did it because he's in love with you, in the most ridiculous, over-the-top, Ethan way possible."

I press my fingers to my temples, inhaling through my nose. "I have spent the last two months in therapy trying to unravel everything that happened, and you want me to just ignore all of it because he loves me? Do you know how messed up that is? That he thought he could trap me in some elaborate lie and I'd just... what? Be grateful? Fall back into his arms? That's not love. That's control."

She's quiet for a long moment, staring down at her coffee. "I think he was just desperate. And desperate people do really, really stupid things."

"Yeah? Well, I was desperate too," I whisper. "Desperate to believe it was real. Desperate to hold onto something, anything, when I thought I had nothing left. And when I finally learned the truth? I felt like I was drowning. Like my own mind wasn't even mine anymore."

Laura closes her eyes briefly, exhaling. "I never wanted that for you. I swear, Hannah. If I could take back my part in it, I would."

I swallow, staring at the ceiling, my vision blurring. "But you can't. None of you can."

We sit quietly for a moment, the heavy air choking our feelings.

"Did none of it feel real?" The question spears my heart and it squeezes in my chest, threatening to suffocate me.

"It felt real, so real."

"I'm not talking about the zombies."

"Neither am I," I say, as tears stream down my face. Laura takes my hand and squeezes it in hers.

"And if none of the other stuff was there, would it have still felt the same?"

I shake out of her grip and stand up. "That's just the thing, I don't know. Did I feel all of it because of the fear, the isolation, the need to have a single soul comforting and understanding, floating with me in a world that's bleak and damaged, or did I feel all of those things because it was Ethan, because it's the way I'd always felt about him?"

That silence grips us again. Laura looks about the room like she's hoping to find an answer on one of my white walls.

"So what now? Are you just going to keep running from him forever?"

"He hurt me—I'm just levelling the playing field."

"Wow, what a great game. Can't wait to see who wins that one."

I ignore her, my jaw tightening. "I don't know. I still have that job offer waiting for me in London."

"The dream job," she swoons.

"Yes!"

"But what about the dream boy?"

"Damnit, I don't know."

"Except that I think you do, Hannah. You always have."

"What did that man do to you?"

"What do you mean?" Her brows furrow and she studies my face.

"You despise Ethan."

She drains the last of her coffee and places the cup near my untouched one. "I hated Ethan for what he did to you, for how he hurt you, but I can respect the extent to which he went to try and win you back, even if it was using the most demented, unhinged method."

I don't respond, and Laura takes that as her cue to close the distance between us. She places a hand on my shoulder and pulls me into her. "Think about it, okay? You love him. I know you do. And yeah, he messed up—big time—but people make mistakes. He knows exactly how much you mean to him. Enough to risk everything, even if it was stupid."

"He is stupid," I mumble, trying to keep some semblance of control, of anger, of victory in my voice, but it's all hollow.

"He'll be gone at the end of the week." She gives me a long hug, one I half-heartedly return. "Don't let your pride get in the way of something amazing."

As she leaves, I sink onto the bed, staring at the pile of unfolded clothes. My heart feels as tangled as the mess in front of me.

I hate the constant state of confusion I've been thrust into.

I hate feeling so uncertain about everything and everyone I know.

I hate that Laura was right about everything but most of all I hate how hopelessly, undeniably, irrevocably I love Ethan Vale.

28. The end of the world

28/01/2026
Ethan

I check my room over one last time. My luggage is packed and ready on the side of the bed, my cupboards empty.

I can run Dad's company from New York; there's no reason for me to stay here now. I did what I could, and she still said no. I've shed the last of the tears I plan to shed for Hannah Jones, if ending the world isn't going to win her back, nothing will.

No more apologies, no more talk, no more explanations. I'm done chasing. I guess she's made up her mind. All that's left now is to run—again. Put as much distance between us as possible and never look back.

It was stupid to come back in the first place, to hold out any hope after all this time. And yet my fingertips ache to feather her smooth skin again, to kiss her full lips, to hear her laughter. I shake the thoughts away and pick up my phone. All that's left is my lift to the airport; the private jet already fuelled and waiting my arrival.

There's a commotion downstairs, but I ignore it—let my mother's '*people*' deal with whatever is going on. But when I hear my mother's distraught screaming, my heart freezes and I turn towards the door just as it bursts open.

On the other side, Frank and Barry, in full zombie getup, are growling and staring at me, their eyes flickering over to my suitcases and back to me. Though they are meant to be dead, I can see the intensity in their eyes—they are very much alive and well—and still hate me. It seeps off them as they take a step closer into my room, Rob and Bruce behind them.

"The gig is done, guys, no need to keep it going, please let yourselves out." I ignore them and get back to my phone, but as I do, they take a few further steps toward me, still growling and snarling in their zombie facade.

"I said you can leave." I stare at them as they advancing. They lunge.

I jump out of the way but there are too many of them. Frank hooks my ankle, and I crash to the floorboards before I can recover. Fingers tangle in my jacket and wrench me sideways; someone pins my legs while another jerks my arms behind me, driving me face-first into the carpet. Plastic bites into my wrists before I can twist free. "What the fuck do you think you're doing?"

I keep getting ignored and I'm yanked off my feet, Frank and Barry grabbing my torso and feet as they carry me out of my room and towards the staircase.

"Let me go!"

I wiggle and twist in their arms, but their hold is iron-clad. Years of mechanical work and physical labour give them strength I do not possess.

I'm hauled like a rag doll down the stairs and carried towards the front door.

In the sitting room I see my mother. She is cowering in her chair, Fiona and Mrs Jenkins growling menacingly at her as she tells them to take what they want and leave her alone. They ignore her and as they see us heading for the door, retreat and follow us out.

"What's going on here?" My tone is sharp as anger spills from my body, part annoyance, part humiliation. "I'm going to end you."

All my threats fall on deaf ears as I get carried out and tossed into the boot of a waiting vehicle.

My bound hands and feet are useless as I try to kick and writhe, screaming profanities at the men taking me so crudely from my home. The car comes to life and in an instant we're moving.

The engine drowns out my threats and angry retorts.

The drive is short, and the noise of the engine dies away, replaced by the opening of car doors. The boot flies open and afternoon sun streams into the small space, blinding me momentarily. Frank and Barry haul me from the boot and slice open the zip ties around my feet.

They each put a hand under my armpits and begin to push me forward, growling.

I check my surroundings and recognition slams into me.

The park has been renovated in the last thirty years, but still, the play equipment is much the same; slides, swings, and a roundabout.

Frank turns to stare, his deadened eyes glaring with something like tolerance. "Just so you know, I'm not doing this for you!" *Or not...* he takes a few extra seconds, as if his glaring eyes are the punctuation at the end of a very obvious statement.

Once he's sure I understand, he cuts the zip ties around my wrists, turns around and taps Barry on the shoulder.

They both walk away over to the knoll behind the small hill, leaving me alone.

The park is eerily quiet, almost too quiet. No yelping of excited dogs, no laughter of playing kids, no screaming of stressed-out parents. I take a few steps, my shoes crunching on the gravel path, and then I see it, a gathering ahead. My heart stutters as I approach. There's a large, ornate archway set up in the middle of the park, decorated with vines and dark, withered roses. But it's not the archway that stops me in my tracks; it's the people.

They're all standing still, facing me, and my stomach twists with unease. Their clothes are torn, their faces pale and sunken with dark circles under their eyes and smears of blood.

The entire town has turned out and they're all in their zombie attire, each one more deformed and disturbing than the next. Sookie has clearly outdone herself yet again. My eyes travel along the sea of people, attempting to comprehend the absurd situation I've been dropped into, and then, I see her.

Hannah.

She's standing right beneath that arch, dressed in a tattered, lace wedding gown, splattered with red. My breath catches in my throat. She's beautiful in a haunting, almost surreal way. My mind struggles to grasp what I'm seeing. My heart swells with love and something else—something like awe.

I can't stop staring at her as I walk forward, the world narrowing to just the two of us. My heart beating wilder with each step.

The guests—the townspeople who usually scowl at me rather than smile—are all here. Frank, Barry, even Bruce. Her parents stand in the aisles, across from them Sookie, arm in arm with a grotesque Angie whose smile stretches hauntingly but full of mirth. I even catch a glimpse of Laura smiling brightly at me. They're all dressed in their best zombie attire—but they become an insignificant blur. It's just Hannah and me now, like it was the first time I saw her here, like it's always been.

As I reach her, my heart thudding so hard it's a wonder she can't hear it. I stare at her, trying to process everything. The eerie setup, the zombie guests, this sudden, unexpected wedding. I finally find my voice, though it's rough with emotion.

"Hi," I breathe a little laugh feeling my throat tighten.

Her nervous eyes meet mine and her smile falters but only a bit "Hi."

"What's going on?"

"Well," She shifts her weight, her voice light and teasing, "you ended the world for me once and I was stupid enough to let you slip away, so I thought I'd return the favour. Turns out you're *officially* the last man on earth... and, honestly, you're not all bad."

My laugh is crazed and elated, all my nerves standing on edge, a mix of relief and disbelief. "Not all bad, huh? High praise."

"Don't let it go to your head," she squeezes my hand. "But yeah, turns out you're the only one I want to spend the end of the world with."

I take her hand, the coolness of her skin meeting my sweaty palm, smearing the paint which makes it look so lifeless. But underneath, I know she's full of life, full of love. The officiant, also zombified, begins the ceremony, but all I can focus on is her.

My heart chugs with wild hope as our vows blur. It's overwhelming, the love I feel for her. When the officiant finally says the words, "You may kiss the bride," I don't hesitate. I pull Hannah close, my mouth crashes into hers, devouring her. The world seems to stand still, and for a second I'm a ten-year-old boy, seeing her for the first time, knowing even then that she'd change my life forever.

Every part of me protests as I pull away from her mouth. "You know, you could've just said you loved me."

She grins, that spark of mischief brighter than ever. "Where's the fun in that?"

Somehow, amid the madness and the mess, we found our way back. This ridiculous, beautiful, end-of-the-world wedding—it's us in every way that matters. And for the first time in forever, everything feels right.

The world could fall apart around us and it still wouldn't matter. Right here, in this strange, perfect place where it all began, I've already found everything I need.

Hannah was never the end of my world; she was only ever my beginning.

Acknowledgments

A Word from Jane.

I really hope you enjoyed this book as much as I enjoyed writing it.

A massive thank you to Tracey Caldwell, who as always, made me see through all the trees when the forest got too thick. Thank you, for all the encouragement, support and feedback all the holes you fixed the errors you found and suggestions that took the book from mediocre to not the worst. To K – As always without your direction, comments and segues my writing will be nowhere near what it is or could be. You drive me to do better and get through the mountain... one day it will actually all happen! Thanks Tyrant x.

Finally, thank you for reading, supporting my work and hopefully enjoying my words, my twisted worlds my broken characters! If you enjoyed the story, please leave a review and recommend the book to any friend you think would love this story. You will have my eternal love and gratitude. Want to know more about the author and keep in touch? get snippets of upcoming books and have a bit of twisted fun?

Come join me in Wonderland.

Also by JA Wynters

Other Books by the author

Guarding Gabriel

Fractured

Mai Tais and Goodbyes

Losing Liam

Four Rooms

The Sweetest Thing

Fractured Fairy tales

Wolf

Beast

Hunter

Dreamer

Liar Liar

Spare Parts

Fixed parts

Broken parts

Coming soon:

Torn apart

Picked apart

Why not leave a review and tell them how much you loved Better Off Dead.

About the Author

Jane Wynters hails from Australia where she lives with her three kids, two fish and one feline companion. She lives on coffee and vodka and loves reading and roller derby.

When she's not keeping her small army alive she loves writing and conjuring new worlds from her imagination.